SHADOW

USA TODAY BESTSELLING AUTHOR
C.J. PINARD

This book is an original publication of Pinard House Publishing.

This is a work of fiction. The names, characters, places, and incidents are products of the writer's imagination or have been used fictitiously and are not to be construed as real. Any resemblance to persons, living or dead, actual events, locales, or organizations is entirely coincidental.

Copyright © 2021-2022 Pinard House Publishing, LLC

This is licensed for your personal enjoyment only. No part of this book may be reproduced, scanned, or distributed in any printed or electronic format without permission. Please do not participate in, or encourage, piracy of copyrighted materials in violation of the author's rights. Purchase only authorized editions.
All rights reserved.

PRINTED IN THE UNITED STATES OF AMERICA

ISBN: 9798753053855

ACKNOWLEDGEMENTS

Cover Art by Kellie Dennis at Book Cover by Design

Copyediting by Amabel Daniels

NIGHTHAWKS MC SERIES

Viper

Shadow

Phoenix

Venom

Face

"Everything that we see is a shadow cast by that which we do not see."

~Martin Luther King, Jr.

1

MISSION OF MURDER

Riding the high of a recent conquest, I killed the engine to my bike and parked behind the clubhouse. Nighthawks' president and founder, Viper, would kill me if he knew what I'd just done. Not that he'd ever caught me before. Just because we were friends—tight like brothers—didn't mean I told him *everything*.

I didn't really consider it keeping secrets, though. It was simply taking care of business. The supernatural problem in Shreveport hadn't been too bad compared to New Orleans. Good God, this place was teeming with monsters. I supposed I was one of them... just not the bad kind.

All right... that came out wrong. I *am* bad. Fuckin' terrible, actually. I just didn't kill without reason or thought. This recent victory was for a good cause, and that cause was getting an evil witch off the streets.

Honestly, it had been too easy. Last week, we'd received an anonymous tip that a woman in the French Quarter was doing "palm readings" and then robbing men of their money. The tip said the human would pay her a hundred bucks to see a glimpse of their future, or communicate with a recently deceased loved one, but after the reading, the men would be knocked out cold and wake up in an alley, missing their wallet and their memory temporarily. Two men, that we know of, never woke up, and their deaths were still unsolved by NOPD. They'd most likely died from whatever the witch had done to knock them out cold. When the ones who survived remembered what happened and eventually went to confront the woman, the shop wasn't there. Or it didn't *appear* to be there. It stunk of magic to me, and there was no way I was going to let this crazy witch get away with this shit.

I ditched the bike at a pay-by-the-hour parking lot and walked to the Quarter, easily finding the "fortuneteller" shop. A woman with too much jewelry and makeup greeted me with a practiced smile on her young-looking face—but I knew she was much older than she looked. She put her hand out to shake mine in greeting, and I declined. Once she touched me, I knew she'd make me, and I couldn't have that. Not yet.

After plunking down a hundred-dollar bill, I said, "I need to contact my dad. He passed last month."

She quickly snatched up the bill and shoved it into her cleavage. "Well, I'm sorry for your loss... uh?"

"Craig," I replied.

"Amara," she said, smiling.

I simply nodded.

"Well, Craig, follow me."

I did as she instructed, and we sat at a small round table with a crystal ball at its center.

Was this chick serious? Real witches didn't use crystal balls. I bit back a smile at the ridiculousness.

"Do you have anything personal of his?" Amara asked.

I shook my head. "No, didn't know I needed it. Do I need to leave?"

She quickly replied, "No, it just makes things easier to have a personal effect." She studied me hard. "What was your father's name?"

"William."

"Okay. May I have a strand of your hair?" she asked.

I plucked one from my beard because I kept my head shaved clean.

She made a face but dumped it into a bowl I'd just noticed on the table. It contained some kind of leafy herbs, and when she threw a lit match into it, it flamed to life briefly before burning small, quiet, and smelly.

I breathed through my mouth. Incense… gah.

She closed her eyes and lifted her hands in the air. "Gods of the afterlife, gods of purgatory, gods of Heaven, gods of Hell. Hear my cry. Let William speak to his son, Craig. Let William's presence be known."

I had to resist an eyeroll.

"Close your eyes, Craig," she commanded.

I did as she instructed but kept one slightly open in a slit to watch her.

Hers fluttered as she mumbled incoherent things that sounded like made-up Latin. After a couple of minutes, she declared she had reached my long-dead father and told me a bunch of crap about how William was explaining to her that they were close and how much he missed me. Blah, blah. Total bullshit obviously, since William hadn't even been my father's name.

"Ask him if Mom's okay," I threw in for shits and giggles.

"William, is your wife with you?" she asked, her eyelids still fluttering.

She waited a few seconds before replying, "Yes, she's happy. They're happy. Together."

Oh, brother.

"Thanks, Amara," I said, opening my eyes and standing up.

"What?" she asked, looking up at me bewildered. "That's it? You don't want to know anything else?"

"Nah, I'm good."

"Sit down, Craig. We're not done," she commanded, almost seeming annoyed.

This must be when she drugged or poisoned her victims to steal their wallets.

I shrugged as if I didn't care and sat back down. "Okay."

"Close your eyes. Your dad has more to say," she commanded.

I bit back a smile. "Cool." I closed them but kept one slitted again.

"He says he's sorry for what he did," she starts. "He loves you very much and regrets his mistakes."

I watched as she took a bottle I hadn't noticed before and squirted it in my direction. It looked like one of those old-timey perfume bottles with the squeeze pump my mother used to use. The mist covered my face, and the scent went up my nose. It stunk but it did absolutely nothing to me.

"Oh, Dad. I forgive you," I said dramatically, playing along. I threw in a couple of sniffs for effect. Then, I plonked my head on the table as if I had passed out.

When I heard and felt the witch get up from her seat and come around behind me, I sat very still. She began lifting my wallet out of my back pocket, and it was then I chose to disappear into thin air.

Witch got parlor tricks? Oh no, babe. *I* got tricks.

Her gasp engulfed the small space, and when I reappeared behind her, she whirled around and glared at me through slitted eyes. "What the hell are you?"

"Your worst nightmare," I replied in my best Hollywood actor voice right before I pulled the buck knife from my belt and sliced clean through her neck. I watched as her head lobbed off and fell to the ground with a thud. Blood flew into my mouth and I licked it off my lips before wiping my eyes with the backs of my hand. I retrieved my wallet and a few hundred-dollar bills from her corpse before strolling out of the shop, whistling the theme to *Bewitched*.

God, I loved that show in the 1960s.

Did I just kill someone for committing robbery? Yep. Did I care? Nope. I was sure she'd done much worse. After all, she was a fucking witch.

Witches… shudder. They gave me the creeps.

I strolled through the door of the clubhouse and saw Phoenix standing by the jail cells talking to Kovah.

"What's up, Shadow?" Kovah asked as I approached. "You look like you've been up to no good." He threw that shit-eating smug smile at me.

"When am I ever up to *actual* good?" I secretly wondered if I still had blood on my face. I'd washed in the witch's bathroom before leaving.

Phoenix laughed and looked down at my shirt. "Never. Better clean off that blood spatter before Viper starts asking questions."

I looked down to see it dried but shiny, microscopic red flecks on the white areas of the design on my black shirt. *Next time: Solid black clothing.* "You never miss anything, do you?"

He raked a hand through his short auburn hair and grinned at me. "No, I really don't."

"So… who'd ya kill?" he asked in a sing-song voice, his eyes wide with curiosity.

"Don't worry about it," I muttered, heading toward my apartment. I was glad Viper had let us have living quarters in this clubhouse because this club was my life. I didn't need another home outside of here since I spent all my time working club business or hanging out at the Cobalt Room, the adjacent nightclub we had bought for extra revenue.

Looking in the mirror in my small bathroom, I could see blood in my beard and all over my T-shirt. My forearms were covered as well, and I made a mental note to wear long sleeves next time I went out on a mission of murder.

"Fuck," I murmured, stripping naked and starting the shower. Once hot, I hopped inside and let the water cleanse me of the witch's blood and of my sins. But would I ever be clean of those? I didn't think so. I'd lived a long time and learned that the only one looking out for me, was me.

"Don't be such a pansy!"

"I'm not being a pansy, Dad. I just don't know what you want

me to do. Where I'm supposed to go."

My father's angry blue eyes narrowed, and his jaw ticked in annoyance. "I said, get! It's time for you to fly the coop, boy. Same as ya' brothers." His Irish brogue more pronounced, which was what happened the angrier he got.

"But I don't want to go," I said, looking at the small brown duffel packed full at my feet. "I don't have a job or anyplace to go."

"Well, ya better find one," he replied, slamming the door in my face.

I stepped off the porch, its wooden slats wailing in protest under my weight.

As I began to walk down the road, I turned one last time to look back at the house I was born in—where I was raised—and wondered what I had done to make my parents so angry. I had watched my older brothers get the same treatment, being kicked out of the family home at eighteen, but I thought being the 'baby', I'd get to stay longer. I guessed that wasn't the case. I saw my mother peering out of the front window, her eyes shiny with tears. I lifted my hand in a wave and she smiled sadly at me.

"I love you, boy," she mouthed at me, blowing me a kiss.

"Love you, Mom," I mouthed back once I could catch my breath.

The curtains went back into place and I turned to look ahead of me at the road leading into town and wondered what the hell I was going to do now.

A ping from my phone broke me out of my memories and I quickly turned off the shower. After wrapping a towel around my waist, I picked up my phone to see a group message from the service Face had set up, alerting us that we had church in ten minutes.

2

BLACK CAT'S OUT OF THE BAG

I stood between Phoenix and Face as Viper commanded the room from the podium inside the Cobalt Room. We were instructed to always have his back as he conducted church, and we never failed to do so.

I watched the way Viper's woman, MyAnna, stared at him with stars in her eyes and I wondered what she saw in the grumpy bastard. What human in their right mind fell in love with a violent fucking monster?

There was no way I'd ever understand it, but it was what it was. Viper protected her like his life depended on it, and I wasn't one to question that. I'd known him for decades and had never seen him like this. I supposed when you found "the one," you just knew. I thought I'd experienced it once, but love for a lifetime just wasn't in the cards for me. Besides... ain't nobody got time for that love and commitment shit.

"Like I said, stay vigilant. I'm getting tips here and there about some unusual witch activity in the area, but nothing to act on as of now. If we get anything substantial, you'll be the first to know." He looked out at the sea of faces seated inside the bar, all the vampires we'd recruited into the club over the past few months. Some had been humans begging to be turned, others had been lost, lone vampires looking for a place to belong. Our numbers now topped over fifty and were either prospects or full-fledged members of the Nighthawks, and I could see the pride beaming from Viper's hazel eyes.

Without any objections or questions, he ended church, and the staff who worked at Cobalt began to prepare for the evening crowd before the doors opened.

"Boss... a word?" I said in Viper's ear as he turned away from the podium.

I watched as Paz, a young, male prospect, whisked the podium away and disappeared into the back office area with it.

"What's up?" Viper asked, once we were semi-alone.

I glanced at his fiancée, who was clinging tightly to his arm, then back to him. "Can we chat alone?"

MyAnna nodded, knowing what was coming. Before Viper could respond, she lifted her chin and untangled herself from her fiancé. "I'll go help Dash behind the bar."

At least she could take a hint.

"What is it, man?" he asked.

"Any word or tips about witches in the Quarter? Or anywhere else?" I asked.

He stared at me hard for a few seconds, and then nodded. "Yeah, one was killed earlier tonight. Lost her head—literally."

I nodded, contemplating what I was going to say next.

"You know, you could just tell me when you go out on a job. You don't have to keep it from me."

I was debating on telling him anyway, but I guessed the proverbial black cat was out of the bag. "Yeah, well, she was stealing from humans and assaulting them... even killed a couple of dudes. I taught her a lesson."

He chuckled. "I'd say she didn't learn much, since you didn't give her a chance to."

I lifted a shoulder and let it fall while stroking my fingers over my beard. "Well, I sent a message at least. Better they just go extinct, anyway. And nobody knows a vampire did it."

"Yeah, but we don't need to start a war. We're trying to keep the peace, so maybe don't go killing witches," Viper quipped, staring at me.

Chuckling, I clapped my friend on the shoulder. "I'll keep that in mind. Someone has to police these witches though, especially ones like that."

"True," he replied, nodding. "That's why New Orleans has us."

"Agreed," I said, bumping his fist with mine.

"Now, next time, just give me a head's up on your solo vigilante missions, will you?" he asked.

I hesitated. I didn't want to be accountable to anyone, but with Vane, I owed him my life and decided he deserved at least that much. "Sure, boss, no worries."

"Stop calling me boss," he said, exasperated.

I chose that moment to disappear into thin air, right before I heard him say, "Stop fucking doing that!"

I materialized in my apartment and found myself at the foot of my bed. A basket of laundry sat on top of it, and I groaned at the thought of folding it and putting it away. Such a mundane task that I would clearly be doing for all of fucking eternity. I dreamed of a world where we didn't have to wear clothes. Why did Eve have to sin in the Garden of Eden and cause us to be ashamed of our nakedness?

Why was I even thinking about this shit? Sunday School lessons from my childhood coming back to haunt me in the most ridiculous way. I pushed the thoughts away and went about my chore. Once that was done, I concentrated briefly until I was in the breakroom inside the clubhouse. I was hungry and in no mood to prowl the streets for a human donor.

"What's up?" I chirped in greeting to Jewel and Fox, who were sipping blood-laden coffee from ceramic mugs with ridiculous sayings on them like *Lady Boss* and *Dracula Wouldn't Judge* on them.

When I opened the freezer to get a blood bag, I could see there was nothing but a few boxes of frozen human snack foods, but no blood. I slammed the door shut and whirled around to the duo sitting at the table. "What the hell, guys?"

"Fox went out to get more," Jewel quickly said, raising her mug to her mouth, her multiple colorful rings glinting from the lights in the breakroom. "There's the wine bottles in the club—"

I had no patience for that and was in the mood for some fresh stuff, anyway.

Concentrating on the donor club down in the Quarter, I soon found myself at the door to Vlad's, the ridiculously cliché vampire bar. Could the owners have made it any more obvious? I supposed it left nothing to the imagination, keeping out the non-vampire supes and inviting in the goth human kids and wannabe vamps.

I wandered inside and gave a discreet sniff in the air. A delicious scent filled my nostrils and I followed it until I found a beautiful blonde standing at the end of the bar, a martini glass with something colorful in it paused at her lips.

"Heya, gorgeous," she said, looking up at me.

With my keen eyesight, I could see she had healed-over bite marks on her neck. But that didn't deter me. If she wanted to be a blood whore, then I was more than willing to be her customer.

"Craig," I said, gripping her waist and pulling her flush against my body.

She giggled and set her drink down. "Kristin. Wow, big man. You sure don't waste any time."

I ground my pelvis into hers so she could feel all of me. "No, I don't." I leaned down and kissed her hard on the mouth, and when her tongue mingled with mine, I groaned against her lips, my cock stiffening even more against her.

Trailing kisses down Kristin's neck, I kept a firm hold on her before I jammed my fangs into her carotid and helped myself to all her deliciously human blood. I whimpered quietly as her essence flowed down my throat and nourished my immortal body.

When I felt her grind her hips into mine, I knew I needed to now sate my *other* needs… and she did not disappoint. In the bathroom of this faux vampire bar, her very talented mouth gave me everything I needed and more.

Thank you, Kristin. You were quite the human feedbag—and more.

Deciding to walk back to the club, I passed an alley and paid it no mind until something in my peripheral vision caught my attention. Mixed colors of light blasted into the air until I was forced to stop and look at what was happening.

"Tell me, leech. Tell me now," I heard a female voice say.

Looking closer, I could see a woman standing over a man, her arm in the air as she wielded enough power to command anyone's attention.

The man whimpered and shook his head. "I don't know, lady. I don't know. Please… let me go. Please…"

"You reek of vampire stench, and I know you leeches stick together. I'll let you go when you tell me who killed Amara."

Alarm bells went off in my head. This crazy witch was looking for whoever had killed the fortuneteller.

Well, that was me.

I looked at the terrified vamp. He was cowering under her magic and I could tell he was a very new vampire.

Act now, save him. Or keep walking.

"Okay, then. Your choice."

I watched as the witch lifted her hand to strike down the new vampire.

"Wait!" I said, my hands out in front of me.

The witch's head whipped in my direction and she narrowed her glowing, purple eyes. "Who are you?"

I lifted my chin. "The one you're looking for."

"Bullshit," she replied quickly, ready to take down the new vampire.

"It's not, though." I put my hands on my hips.

She raised her hand as if to strike down the new vampire. Then, she looked at me.

Shrugging casually, even though I was on edge, I said, "I don't care if you kill him or not, but it will be all for nothing."

She lowered her hand, and that was all the opportunity the young vampire needed. He used preternatural speed to exit the alley, leaving me alone with the witch.

"You're welcome," I called out sarcastically to his retreating figure.

She watched briefly as he left, then narrowed her eyes at me. I had my arms folded across my cut and I saw her eye it before looking up at me. I was still about ten feet away from her, acting aloof but ready to defend myself.

"Stop doing magic out in the open," I snapped.

"Why did you kill Amara?" she asked, ignoring my demand.

I snorted. "Because she was killing human men and stealing from them."

The witch was young, not just young-looking, with flaming red curls cut short and dressed like a video game heroine in tight black leather. I found this curious, since witches dressed like hippies. She wore high-heeled boots and I wondered how fast she could run with them.

"She was doing no such thing, vampire," she hissed at me.

Chuckling, I said, "Wanna bet?"

The colorful magic dripping from her fingers began to fade and she stood at full height, now seeming more curious than angry. "Tell me." She folded her arms across her chest.

"What more do you want to know? I've told you why I killed her. Now, keep your magic hidden so the Nighthawks won't have to declare open season on witches. Feel me?"

"Open season…" She threw her head back and laughed. "Are you insane? We can kill you all with a snap of our fingers." She posed with one hand in the air, her fingers ready to snap.

I laughed again. "No, you can't."

She obviously thought I knew nothing about witches. Cute.

"What's your name?" I asked, not sure why that came out of my mouth.

"Why do you want to know? So you can hunt me down and kill me?"

"If I wanted you dead, you'd already be headless, just like your friend," I quipped.

She made a face. "You're reprehensible and disgusting. Filthy vampire."

"I'm Shadow," I said, trying to get her to talk.

Why was I trying to get her to talk?

"I can read," she snarked, pointing at my cut.

I didn't care for this bitch's attitude, so I simply mimicked her pose and snapped my fingers, disappearing before her eyes, her gasp the last thing I heard before I materialized inside the clubhouse.

3

WITCHY WOMAN

"Geez! Would you not do that?" Venom snapped, startling at "Gotta keep you on your paws." I chuckled, nudging the wolf in the arm.

He took a bite of pizza he had folded in his hand and looked down at something on his phone. "Everyone's on edge enough around here, you asshole."

I laughed because he said it around a mouthful of food.

"You're fuckin' gross," I replied, walking toward the walkway that led to the Cobalt Room.

"Pot, meet kettle," he murmured.

I made my way into the club and found Kovah and Face standing around talking and drinking.

"What's up?" I asked.

"Where you been?" Kovah inquired, a beer paused at his mouth.

I relayed the story about where I'd been.

"That's pretty powerful magic if you can see it," Face replied.

"Yeah, that's why I think we may have a problem on our hands." I blew out a breath.

Kovah laughed. "Witches… if they're all female, then they're all problems."

I shook my head. "You're not wrong but there are some males

in the mix." I looked around the club. "Where's Viper?"

Face jutted his thumb behind him. "Office."

I made my way down the hall and stopped at his door. "Knock, knock," I said, rapping on the doorframe.

"Come in," Viper said, but I had already started making my way to the chair in front of his desk.

"I just went down to Vlad's to feed and on my way back I caught a witch threatening a baby vamp in one of the alleys. She was using colorful magic, and aside from being in the alley, she wasn't being very subtle about it."

He leaned forward, his hands on the desk. "Why was she threatening him?"

I proceeded to relay the entire event to him.

"She never told you her name?" he asked, now leaning back in his chair with his arms behind his head.

I shook my head. "Nope. I'll find her, though. She doesn't look like a normal witch. I just wanted to let you know we might have a witch problem on our hands soon."

"I get that you were trying to save the vamp, but you shouldn't have admitted it was you who killed the other." He stared hard at me.

I waved a hand. "Don't do that. I know what I'm doing. I'll find her and give her the same sendoff Amara got."

"Just chill," Viper replied, hands up. "No need to kill her. It'll start an all-out war."

I waggled my eyebrows. "And...?"

"Violent fucker," he muttered under his breath, putting his attention back on the screen.

"Violence is my middle name," I said.

"No, your middle name is Andrew. Stop it. We don't need a war. We're here to keep the peace. Just find the witch, talk to her. Don't hurt her and don't kill her. You dig?"

I stood and nodded. "Yeah, but you're no fun."

"I'm always the life of the party," he groused, looking back at the computer.

Scoffing, I walked out of his office and up to my apartment. I threw my cut onto the bed and removed the chains I wore around my belt. In just a black tee and dark jeans and boots, I materialized back into the Quarter to find this witch. It wasn't like I had much else going on. The others could hold down the club for the night.

My first thought was to go right back to the alley, but of course she wasn't there. I began walking, blending in with the tourists and young adults carrying drinks and getting wasted. I breathed through my mouth because of the overpowering smell of human piss that filled my nostrils.

Making my way back to the fortuneteller's shop, I could see yellow police tape covering the door. Looking both ways to see if anyone was watching, I was relieved to seem to be oblivious to the partygoers. I quickly yanked off the tape and stepped inside the shop. It was quiet and dark, and I didn't sense or smell anyone else around.

I could see the dark stain on the linoleum floor where someone had attempted to clean up the witch's blood. Her body was, of course, gone, but nothing looked different than it had from a couple of nights ago when I'd been here.

A large black book on a nearby table caught my eye and I went over it to. *Necromancy* it read on the cover.

Shudder.

I began rifling through drawers, hoping to find a smaller black book or anything with a list of contacts in it. I would go through every name on there until I found this smart-mouthed redhead and let her know not to fuck with the Nighthawks or any vampire for that matter.

Mostly trinkets I didn't dare touch and junk were found during my search, so I wandered further into the shop and came upon a small bedroom. Hippie-witch clothes hung in the small closet and on top of a dresser sat a lot of jewelry and makeup. I started going through drawers and found nothing but more clothing and more junk.

"Fuckin' packrat," I muttered as I stood in the room and looked around. A full-sized bed with a colorful, gawdy bedspread took up most of the room. I did another search of the closet and found a shoebox on the top shelf. I pulled it down and set it on the dresser. Inside were a bunch of papers, and I began searching through them, not finding much except receipts and bills.

I put the lid back on the box and replaced it into the closet. As I was leaving the bedroom, the strong scent of lilacs hit me, and I stiffened in alarm.

Witches.

As I walked out into the main shop area, I froze when I saw a dark figure standing in the doorway to the shop, blocking my exit. Not that I needed to use the front door, but it seemed I'd found what I was looking for. Or rather, she'd found me.

"What the fuck are you doing in here, vampire?" she hissed.

I looked down to see that rainbow-colored magic dripping from her fingers. When it hit the floor like liquid, it dissipated into nothing. Strange.

I looked back into the redhead's face and said, "I was looking for you."

"Why?" she asked, her fingers twitching.

"Because." I took a step toward her. "I need to talk—"

She lifted both hands out in front of her and blasted her magic at me. It hit me in the chest, and I went flying backward, through the bedroom door, and landed on my back on the bed. I went to get up, but she jumped on top of me, straddling my stomach.

I could easily overpower her and push her off, but I didn't. I put my hands behind my head, laced my fingers together, and grinned into her angry face. "Playful witch."

"Nosy vampire," she countered, narrowing her eyes as she stared down at me. Her red curls curtained her face, but it was cut short, so it stopped at about her chin length.

Why was I paying so much attention to this chick? This witch?

"Not nosy. Like I said, looking for you."

"Why?" she hissed.

"We need to talk," I said. Then I waggled my eyebrows and assessed her from her legs, up her torso, to her tits, then up into her eyes, "Unless you'd rather do something else."

Now, I always went out of my way to ensure I didn't fuck any witches. They were crazy and unpredictable. I stuck to willing humans and sometimes female vampires. But I would be willing to give this one a run for her money.

"Ew," she replied, jumping off me. She stood in the doorway of the room and watched as I got up off the bed.

I chuckled and straightened out my wrinkled shirt. Then I looked up at her. "What's your name?"

She closed her mouth and licked her teeth before raising her chin. She hesitated a few more long seconds, so I just waited before she finally replied, "Bloome."

"Well, Bloome, I come in peace." I bowed for effect.

She narrowed her eyes at me. "No, you don't. You killed Amara." She jutted her thumb behind her at the shop.

"Nighthawks don't fuck around, sweetheart. Let the rest of your coven, or whatever you witches have going on, know that they're not gonna get away with shit. Do your magic in private, don't expose yourselves to humans unless you're doing tricks for money or whatever you do to support yourselves. And absolutely *no* killing. We clear?"

She made a scoffing noise and chuckled. "We don't work for

you. We don't report to you. We do whatever the hell we want."

I used vampire speed to close the short distance between us and yanked her hair back as she gasped. Inches from her face, I said, "No, you do *not* do whatever the hell you want. If you wish, your witch friends can have an audience with us, and we'll listen to whatever you have to say."

"Let go of me!" she screeched.

I hissed when she used magic to zap the hand that held her hair back. I let go and seethed at her, "Do not do that again."

"Don't touch me, you leech," she snapped, stepping back with magic sparking and dripping from her fingertips once again.

We stared at each other for what seemed like forever before I brushed past her and found a piece of paper and a pen. I wrote down the phone number to the repair shop at the clubhouse and told her to ask for me if she wanted to meet with us. "To straighten things out and lay down some ground rules."

She laughed. "We've been in New Orleans for a couple of centuries, and we don't answer to vampires. Ever. So take your little biker club and shove it up your—"

Before she could finish, I gripped her hair back and slammed my mouth down on hers, kissing her hard and fast.

After I broke the kiss, she blinked shocked blue eyes at me and panted hard.

"It was the only way to shut you up."

She reached up and slapped me, but of course it felt more like a tickle, especially since she caught mostly beard.

I chuckled. "Have a pleasant evening, Bloome."

I disappeared as I heard her scream in frustration.

4

BLOOD MOON

I materialized in the walkway to the club and went back inside to find the guys right where I left them. Now, Phoenix had joined them. I noticed Viper and MyAnna sat at a table talking to some of the prospects.

Kovah assessed my clothing and asked, "Where have you been?"

I looked down and realized I forgot to put my cut on. Looking around to ensure nobody was watching me, I disappeared, materialized into my bedroom, threw on the cut, and reappeared in the hallways near the bathrooms of the club. I walked back out wearing it.

"To answer your question," I said, re-joining them, "I was in the Quarter. Witch hunting."

"I didn't realize it was open season on witches. Sounds like fun," Kovah replied.

I laughed. "It's not. I was looking for one in particular."

Face set his drink down and leaned his elbow on the bar. "The one from the alley."

I nodded. "Yep."

"So, did you find her tonight?" Face asked.

"Yep."

"And...?" Kovah snapped.

I told them what happened as Dash set my drink in front me. I thanked him and downed it in one gulp. "Ah, smooth."

"You kissed the bitch? Are you insane? She could have burned your lips off," Face said.

I shrugged one shoulder. "Yeah, I guess so. But she didn't put up too much of a fight."

"Sounds hot," Phoenix commented.

"She's a redhead. Like you. Y'all crazy. All of you," I replied, staring at my fire-wielding brother.

"Yeah, I'd stay far away then," Kovah said. No surprise there, he hated redheads because the blue-eyed human ones became succubus vampires once turned.

"You exchange numbers?" Phoenix asked.

I chuckled. "No, it's not like that. I did give her the number to the shop, though. Told her to ask for me if she or her coven wanted to talk to us."

"Yeah, don't hold your breath," Face muttered. "Witches hate vamps."

"Feeling's mutual," Phoenix commented.

"Fuck," I heard Face swear.

We all turned to where he was looking to see the damn BSI cops walk in.

"The fuck do they want?" Phoenix asked, scowling at the pair. He hated the BSI, but I had yet to get the scoop as to why.

We watched as they approached Viper at the table. The male and female agents said something too low for us to hear and then they turned and looked at me as Viper pointed at me.

The three of them walked toward us.

"Agents," Kovah said in his best smartass tone. He even bowed.

"Stop it," Agent Bishop said, biting back a smile. He gave Kovah a fist-bump. I knew those two went way back, and I'd have to get the story sometime.

"Do you want to go someplace quieter and talk, Mr. Walsh?"

"You can call me Shadow, or Craig, and no, here is good."

Agent Shields pulled her notepad out and began scribbling something. Then she looked up at me with her big brown eyes. "The dead witch in the Quarter from last night. That was you?"

I folded my arms across my chest and asked, "Why?"

"Just tying up loose ends is all," she replied.

"I thought you only cared if we killed or hurt humans. Or those damn faerie people you guys like to protect."

She nodded her head. "While that's true, we still have to keep detailed records of supe-on-supe violence. It helps us keep track of things."

I glanced around at my club brothers, and they mostly shrugged, not sure what I should tell the agents. Viper nodded slightly at me to go ahead. I looked at Agent Shields. "I'll talk to you as long as you give me your word that you're not gonna haul me off to that island jail of yours."

Agent Bishop chuckled. "No, we won't be doing that."

I stared hard at him for a few seconds and said, "Yeah, it was me. She was robbing and assaulting human men. Killed a couple. I took care of a problem. That's it."

Bishop thumb-typed into his phone while Shields scribbled in her notebook. She actually got done quicker than Bishop.

"I don't suggest murder, Mr. Walsh," Agent Shields replied, ignoring my previous request to not be called that. "Next time call us. We'll address the problem."

I wanted to laugh but refrained. "Okay."

I *so* wasn't calling the "cops" next time I had problem. The Nighthawks were more than capable of taking care of shit. But I'd tell these fuckers what they wanted to hear if it made them go away.

"Have a good evening, gentlemen," Agent Bishop said, walking way. Then he turned to Kovah and said in hushed tones he probably thought we couldn't hear, "Let's do drinks. I have news."

Kovah fist-bumped him and the agents left the bar.

"What kind of news?" I asked Kovah to annoy him.

He lifted the beer to his lips and turned his face toward me. I couldn't tell if he was looking at me because of those damn shades he wore. "Oh, his wife is probably pregnant again. They have two ankle biters already."

"You two tight?" I asked, signaling Dash over to the bar for a drink.

"The usual?" he asked.

"Bourbon," I replied, tapping the bar in thanks to him.

"We go back a ways," Kovah replied. "Long before he was an agent."

I nodded and didn't ask him anything more.

"Shit," Face said, and we turned to look at him. "Just got an alert from the police blotter about some tourists who were attacked in the Garden District."

"So?" I replied.

He looked up from his phone and said to me, "They said a wolf jumped out at them." He looked back down at the phone and began to read, "The wolf, described as white and gray, snarled at them and then pounced. The man and woman suffered multiple lacerations about the throat, shoulders, and arms, and were taken to West Jefferson ER."

"But it's not even a full moon," I said, checking my phone's calendar.

"That's what I was about to say," Phoenix commented.

"Does it say what happened to the wolves?" Viper asked, pointing to Face's phone.

He read some more. "The couple reports the animals ran off when the man pulled a knife from his pants pocket and threatened the wolves with it. Then, they called nine-one-one."

"So not actual wolves. Werewolves," Viper said, sounding

annoyed.

"Maybe we should let the BSI handle this," Kovah said. "I'm sure they've heard about it already."

Viper shook his head. "No. Fuck no. These mutts need to know we aren't fuckin' around. They've all been warned. These packs can't keep a leash on their pups, then we're going to keep teaching them a lesson until they get it through their thick skulls." He looked around the bar, then back to us. "Where's Venom?"

"Good question. I'll go find him." I took a quick look around and disappeared, materializing inside the warehouse.

I gasped when I saw Venom in his wolf form, wandering around like a pet dog.

"What the fuck?" I said to the wolf.

He just looked at me, and in his eyes, he looked frightened. We had been locking him up during the full moon since his inception into the club, for his protection and ours, but for the past three months, he'd been cautiously allowed to roam the clubhouse in his wolf form. He slept in one of the cells at night, where he kept a pair of shorts, food, and water, and transitioned back to human each day when the sun came up. He was clearly not prepared this time, as there were no supplies in the cell. I looked at my phone's calendar again. The full moon wasn't for two more days.

"What the hell is going on?" I asked Jewel as she and Fox emerged from the breakroom. Their eyes were wide as they stared at Venom.

"I… I don't know, boss. We heard you come in and we're just as confused as you are," Jewel answered.

Fox looked at his watch then to me with concern in his dark-brown eyes. "Full moon's not for two more days."

"Exactly my point. Fuckin' sucks we can't ask him what's going on." I pointed at Venom, who sat on his haunches with his tongue hanging out, looking at us as if we had the answers.

"Well, get him set up with some clothes and food and water. Looks like he'll be in the cage tonight."

"You got it," Fox replied, heading toward the breakroom.

"This is so weird," Jewel replied, chewing her fingernail, her rings shining under the lights.

I thought of something. "I'll be right back."

I ran toward the front door of the clubhouse and the familiar beeping of the door let me know the alarm was still armed. I raced into the parking lot and looked up at the moon. It was almost full, of course, but not a perfect circle. Then, I looked closer, squinting my eyes at it. It had a reddish hue to it, something I hadn't seen in a couple of years. I jogged next door and went into the Cobalt Room through the front door.

I looked at Face. "Blood moon."

He nodded. "Yeah, I saw. They aren't that rare, though. However," he continued, reading on his phone, "we can only see it in the Northern Hemisphere occasionally. So that makes me think the blood moon only affects the wolves when it can be seen."

"How come we didn't know about this?" I asked.

"I think we just forgot. It's happened before," Viper said, looking at me.

"That's right. It has. We should have been prepared."

Face pocketed the phone. "Let me check on Venom."

I grabbed his shoulder. "Already did. He's a wolf. I've got Jewel and Dash getting his cell ready for tonight."

Viper jutted his chin toward the clubhouse and said to Face, "Go let Venom know what's going on. He's probably scared and confused."

I chuckled. "He is."

I really shouldn't laugh. I could attest to the fact that there was nothing worse than being frightened out of your mind and not knowing what was going on with your own body.

HOLE IN MY SOUL

Bay City, Michigan – 1951

I couldn't believe my parents just booted me out like that. My two older brothers, Elliot and Colin, had been gone for over five years and had gotten married and started families. We saw them often, as they still lived in Bay City, and I told myself that they had done all right, and so would I. I just needed some time to get on my feet. I just wished they'd given me a warning.

"What kind of warning did you want, boy? Your brothers were out at eighteen. Did ya think you were some kinda special, or what?" my dad said as I begged my parents to let me stay and get my affairs in order before leaving the family home.

"Well, uh, no… I just thought I'd have more time," I replied.

"Ya schoolin' was done three months ago, boy, and now you're a man. It's time for you to be on ya own, son. You'll be all right."

I looked at my mom and she was close to tears. She laid a hand on my father's meaty forearm and looked up at him. "Can't he stay, Joe? Just a few months until he gets himself a job and such?"

Her Irish brogue sounded so much lovelier coming out of her mouth than it did my dad's.

He shook his head. "Kid's gotta fly the coop, Aoife. You know how it goes."

She nodded and pulled me into a hug. "I love you, Craig. If ya need anything, ya come back here and see us, all right?"

My father shot her a look and shook my hand. "Go out and do great things, boy."

My parents had been nice enough to give me fifty dollars, but I knew it wouldn't last.

I thought about going to Colin's house and asking to crash but he was just as much of a jerk as Dad and figured he'd probably tell me to go pound gravel. He lived in a tiny house with his wife and two kids. But I'd sleep on the floor at this point, just until I could get a plan going.

I found myself heading toward the woods, knowing good and well I shouldn't be. There were wild animals, but thankfully, winter hadn't come yet. I shuddered to think about what would happen then if I didn't find shelter.

Using the skills I'd learned in the Boy Scouts, I spent most of the day and into the evening collecting tree branches and other things to create a shelter. Tomorrow, I would go into town and find a job—pray someone would hire me.

I shivered as the cool September night set in. I'd put on three pairs of clothes and managed to set a small fire to keep warm. Mom had snuck a few bowls of her stew into my backpack, and judging by how much I had, it would last about three days, if that. And that was if I only ate once a day. I snuggled down on the soft dirt and pine needle bed I'd made and was able to drift off into a fitful sleep, every little branch cracking and animal noise waking me.

I woke the next day and took off two layers of clothes. I found a stream nearby and filled my canteen, trying to brush my teeth as best I could with my finger and some soap.

"So disgusting," I murmured, spitting into the stream and rinsing my mouth with the ice-cold, clean water.

I left the makeshift shelter intact and threw dirt on the remaining embers of the fire before walking out of the forest and toward town.

A new hotel had been built a few years' prior and that was my first stop. I wanted to see how much they would charge for a couple nights' stay, because I sure as heck was not going to live in the woods.

The walk took me almost two hours, but when I reached the hotel, I was delighted to see a "help wanted" sign on the front door. I quickly made my way to the front desk.

"Hello, I'm inquiring about your help wanted sign?" I said, smiling as charmingly as I could at the pretty lady working the desk.

"Sure, let me get the manager. Stay here," she replied, smiling back at me.

A man about my dad's age dressed in an impeccable suit and shiny shoes came out to greet me. "Hello, young man." He put his hand out to shake and I reciprocated.

"Hi, I'm Craig Walsh. I'm looking for work," I replied, smiling.

"I'm Ralph Johnson. Follow me," he said, leading me behind the reception desk and into an office. "Please, sit." He indicated a chair, and I did as I was told.

"Do you have any work experience?" he asked, sitting behind the desk.

I shook my head. "No, I'm afraid not, sir. Just graduated high school, looking for my first job. I'll do anything, just so you know. I just need to earn some money so I can get a place of my own."

He regarded me carefully and said, "You look awfully young. Do you not still live with your folks?"

I shook my head. "No, they told me I was better off on my own." I put on a practiced smile I was hoping he couldn't see right through. "So, here I am."

"I see." He looked down at his desk and ruffled through some papers. "We have three positions. One is a dishwasher for the hotel's kitchen. The other is janitorial—you will assist Martha in cleaning all aspects of the hotel, aside from the guest rooms. The third is a mechanical position. Repairing and replacing things that break or need to be upgraded. Stuff of that nature. George is our lead handyman. You'll report to him."

"My dad and I used to repair things around the house all the time. I've replaced windows, doors, flooring, heck, even car parts. I'd like to think I'm pretty handy with a hammer and a wrench." I smiled again at him.

"Very well. Sounds like you'd be good with repairs and maintenance. It pays a dollar sixty-five an hour and you'll be required to work no less than thirty hours per week. How does that sound?"

My stomach turned over as nerves and excitement erupted in me. "I'll take it, Mr. Johnson!"

"Very well, be here tomorrow at eight a.m. sharp and I'll have George show you the ropes."

I stood and shook his hand again. "You won't be disappointed, sir!"

After leaving his office, I wandered out into the reception area and asked the pretty clerk about rates.

"Our basic room is three dollars per night," she replied.

I contemplated this carefully. I had fifty dollars to last me until my first paycheck. When would that be?

Embarrassed, I asked her, "Um. When do you get paid?"

Her smile faded and she looked at me, confused. "I beg your pardon?"

I smacked my palm to my forehead. "I'm so sorry. That came out wrong, ma'am. I just got hired. When can I expect my first paycheck?"

She visibly relaxed. "Oh. Well, congratulations. We get paid every two weeks. Just got paid yesterday, so two weeks for you if you start Monday."

"Very well, thank you."

I turned and walked out. I'd spend a couple more nights in the woods and then see what I could work out with Mr. Johnson as far as accommodations. Three dollars a night would eat up my fifty bucks fast, and I didn't want to squander it.

"Boy, give me that!" George said, snatching the wrench out of my hand.

I was covered in smelly water from trying to fix a pipe that had burst in one of the guest rooms' bathrooms. Sliding out from under the sink, I suppressed a gag as I was covered in putrid water. How did someone clog a sink so absolute?

George, a cranky but easygoing man in his fifties, slid under the sink and put the wrench to the pipe. "Pay attention, son."

I did as he instructed, watching as he quickly loosened the pipe. All the water went gushing into a small bucket he'd placed under it. We spent the next half hour cleaning out the pipes and putting the project back together.

"Good job," George said proudly. "It's really not hard work, once you learn everything. I'm self-taught and I'll teach you everything I know, if you're willin'."

I nodded. "I am."

He packed up his tool bag and we stood to leave.

"Hey," I said as we exited the room. "Do you live here, or do you have your own place?"

"Got a wife and two grown sons, I live a few blocks from here. Why?"

"I don't have any place to stay. Been camping out in the woods, was hoping we could get a discount on a room for working here. It's gonna take me months to save up for a room to rent."

George looked alarmed and said, "Your folks dead or something?"

I shook my head. "Nah, they just don't allow their kids to live at home past eighteen. I mean, I knew it was coming, but thought since I was the youngest they'd make an exception. Nope! Booted me out three days ago with fifty bucks and a hug. Happy birthday to me, right?"

"Tough break, kid," he replied, shaking his head. "I don't think Johnson allows us to live in the hotel but lemme talk to the missus and see if we can't rent ya a room. My boys are married and have their own families. We got room."

I instantly relaxed. "That would be swell. Thanks, George!"

He placed a hand on my shoulder. "No problem."

I went back to my tent in the woods and prayed that his wife would agree to it. Otherwise, I'd better get comfortable here.

Or beg my parents to let me move back in and pay them rent or something.

The next day, George informed me his youngest son lost his job and he and his family would have to move back in with them temporarily, but he did know a guy renting a room above his garage and would only charge me twenty-five dollars a month.

"You don't smoke, do you, kid?"

I shook my head. I barely had enough money for food, let alone cigarettes.

"Good, 'cause Alfie don't want no smokers and no partiers. You gotta stay quiet. Guy works nights so he sleeps during the day."

I snorted. "Not a problem. I have friends, but we don't talk much. They're either gettin' married or joinin' the service."

George put his hand out and I handed him another nail. He lined it up with the cabinet door and began hammering. "What are you gonna do with your life, kid?"

I shrugged. "I have no stinkin' clue. I hope to get enough experience working here so that I can apply at the factory. I know they pay pretty well. Then I'll decide from there, I guess." I handed him another nail.

"Not a bad plan," he replied over the sound of the hammer.

After our workday was done, he wrote down directions to Alfie's place and I wasted no time walking the ten blocks there.

This walk is going to suck in the winter.

The house wasn't in the best shape, but it looked fairly new, and I wasn't picky. I rang the doorbell.

A man dressed in a nice suit and a clean haircut answered the door. He looked really pale but then I remembered George saying he worked nights so he must sleep during the day.

"Hello, you must be Craig. I'm Alfred, please come in."

I took my hat off and stepped inside. "Thank you."

"Follow me," he said.

He led me through the house and up a staircase. At the top was a door. He unlocked it with a key, and I found it odd that the lock was on the outside of the door. I assumed he'd give me the key once I moved in.

The door opened up into a large attic space with one small window on the far wall. There was a bed, a wardrobe, and a mirror attached to the wall. Nothing else took up the space. There was room for at least three beds and three wardrobes, so I was happy with the large space.

"This is very nice, sir. The furniture comes with? I don't have any."

He nodded. "Yes, of course. Do you think these accommodations will work for you?"

Smiling, I said, "Yes, absolutely. May I move in tonight?"

He chuckled and handed me the key. "Yes. George already paid half the rent for the month for you, so just give me the other half when you get paid, or by the end of the month, and we'll be square."

He put his hand out to shake and I took it, pumping it up and down. "Thank you so much!"

"Of course. Just a couple of rules, though. No smoking or drinking, and please try to stay quiet. I'm aware you work during the day, but I do sleep, as my job requires me to be up at night. So, I'll be in and out at night, but on the weekends, I'm aware you will be here during the day."

"It won't be a problem. I'm a pretty boring guy," I said, laughing nervously.

"Good," he replied with a wink. "Now if you need to go get your things, go ahead. The other key on that chain is to the front door. Please keep it locked at all times, whether you're here or not."

I found this odd. We never locked our doors when I lived at home, but maybe this guy was hiding valuables or something in here. I wasn't one to question him, especially since he'd been so generous, so I simply replied, "Yes, sir."

After shoving the key into the pocket of my trousers, I made the walk to the forest to retrieve my meager belongings and move into my new place. I tried to think of a way to pay George back, as well. That was very kind of him.

I was thanking God for the kindness of strangers and friends alike today.

COVEN CHAOS

I stared incredulously at Venom. "You think I'm scared?"

"Absolutely not," he replied, the hot dog paused at his mouth. "I'm just saying, we're much stronger during the blood moon."

"And apparently much more stupid," I murmured.

"Not stupid, but crazy. Probably why those wolves attacked those humans. We can be impulsive but know our boundaries."

Phoenix snorted. "Right. Remember those ones in the Quarter a few months ago we had to get rid of? There was no blood moon then. So what was their excuse?"

Venom swallowed the last of his bite and said, "The whole pack went crazy. I thought we went over this."

Shaking my head, I said, "That's not an explanation, though. Just that one pack happened to go mad? Because there have been plenty of wolf attacks over the course of my lifetime I could tell you about."

"Same," Viper replied, standing next to me, his arms folded across his chest.

Venom ran a hand over his mouth and down his salt-and-pepper beard to clear all the crap that had fallen off his bread-wrapped hot dog. "Like humans, there are deviants among us. Some are born bad and don't give a fuck about the rules. If we were all insane, we certainly wouldn't still be a secret to the humans. We'd be attacking constantly during a full moon."

He had a point.

"Fine. So, what's your take on this wolf issue now?"

With a shrug, he said, "Let's get out and find them."

"What do you mean 'let's'? Is there a mouse in your pocket?" Phoenix asked, laughing.

"Fuck you, fire boy. You guys go find him. I'll be in my cage licking my balls." Venom flipped him off.

"Ew," MyAnna said, coming up to Viper and putting her arms around his waist.

"Sorry, girl. Didn't smell ya comin'," Venom replied with a tip of his invisible hat.

She rolled her eyes and smiled. "I was just kiddin'. I'm used to you boys' filthy talk by now," she drawled.

"You heading out?" Viper asked her, looking down at her with that look in his eyes that I didn't think I'd ever get used to. Kinda made me want to gag, to be honest. I'd known the man thirty years and had never seen him like this.

"Yes, class starts in twenty."

I just now noticed her workout clothing.

"You're not going alone." He didn't ask.

"Jewel's coming," she replied, grinning as she reached up on tiptoe to kiss him.

I snorted out a laugh as I saw Jewel coming out from her apartment before sprinting down the stairs. She wore some tight, shiny black yoga pants and a tank top with a big mouth sporting vampire teeth dripping blood from them. She had none of her jewelry on and her hair up in some bun thing on the top of her head.

"Subtle," Viper muttered, nodding his head at her shirt.

"Love you!" MyAnna called out before they left out the front door.

"You're gonna owe Jewel big time," I said, biting back a laugh.

"I know," he groused.

"Shadow!"

We all turned to see Paz, one of the prospect mechanics, poke his head out of the door leading to the shop.

"Yeah?" I asked.

"Got a phone call." He raised the cordless phone into the air.

I heard Face and Phoenix chuckling. They knew as well as I did who it was. Everyone else I knew had my cell phone.

Hell, everyone else I knew was standing in this room. I had no friends except them. And I sure as hell had no family.

"Shadow," I answered after taking the phone from Paz's hand.

"This is Bloome. My sisters and I would like to meet with you and your vampires. Is tonight good?"

I checked my watch to see it was barely past 7 p.m. "Sure, meet us at the Cobalt Room on Twenty-First Street in half an hour."

"I'm not sure I can round them up in half an hour."

"Then you don't want that meeting very badly, do ya, sweetheart?"

I heard her huff dramatically in irritation.

I pursed my lips together to keep from laughing.

"See you then." She hung up.

After putting the greasy fingerprinted phone back onto the cradle on the wall, I went back out into the clubhouse. Venom, as his wolf, sat curled up in his cell.

"Witches are stopping by in about thirty minutes. Told her to meet us in the club."

"Okay, lieutenants only. Let's get things ready," Viper said, heading toward the walkway that led to the club, and we followed. "Text Kovah," he added, to no one in particular.

I looked at Face and Phoenix and said, "I got it."

Me: *Emergency meeting in 20*

It took him three minutes to reply.

Kovah: *I'll be there*

"Kovah's good," I replied once we had set up the tables the way we wanted.

I poured three glasses of blood from the wine bottle blood section of the bar and sat down with my brothers. I handed Phoenix and Face their glasses. Viper got his blood straight from the tap these days and obviously never needed the bottled stuff.

It was a stash I was responsible for keeping up with. Since I could appear and disappear, I'd been tasked with taking blood bags from the local donation center. I wasn't sure how they even kept up their supply, since I wasn't the only vampire in the area who did this. The poor humans in New Orleans who actually needed blood transfusions had to wait a while for blood because of this. I paid karma back by sneaking into hospital rooms and feeding dying humans my blood to help heal them. It wasn't ideal, and was definitely risky, but I was always the one who felt like there was a circle of life and that karma was a real fucking bitch.

"Did she say how many she was bringing?" Viper asked when the conversation stalled.

I shook my head. "Nope. How many witches are in coven, anyway?"

"A coven is anywhere from three to a hundred," Phoenix replied immediately.

Face stopped thumb-typing on his phone and looked at him. "Oh, that's just awesome."

I chuckled. "I doubt she'd—"

Just then, the front door opened and in walked Bloome, flanked by four women and one man. He was almost as effeminate as they were.

Five it is.

"Have a seat," Face said, standing to greet them. Once they sat, he asked, "Drinks? Sorry, we don't serve food here."

Bloome made a scoffing sound. "Shocking."

I narrowed my eyes at her. "Have some respect."

Viper cleared his throat. "What can we do for you?" he asked.

"I'll take a gin and tonic," one of the witches replied, looking at Face with a flirtatious smirk. She was pretty, blonde ringlets on her head, porcelain skin, big crystal-blue eyes.

"Noted," he said. "Anyone else?"

"Wine, please," the male replied.

The rest of them shook their heads.

I turned briefly to see Face preparing the drinks, then I looked back at Viper.

"We'd like to set down some ground rules," he started. "We're well aware that the Nighthawks are new around here, but we're not new in general."

"Let me guess, you're, like, a thousand years old?" Bloome offered with a facetious smirk on her face.

I scowled at her. "His age is none of your business, red."

"Neither is my hair color, yours. Don't call me that," she seethed.

Face set the drinks down then took his seat.

I blew her a kiss.

Bloome flipped me off, and by the look on her irate yet curious face, I knew I had gotten under her skin. Although she seemed to partly enjoy it.

"Okay, red… what can we do for you and your clan?"

"It's Bloome. That's my name, asshole." She lifted her chin.

"I highly doubt that," I said, laughing.

"Let's get back to the issue at hand…" Viper sounded annoyed.

I ignored him.

"Bloome, really? Your mom was a hippie, or what?" I asked,

smirking at the redhead whose clothes I wanted to tear off. I would bet she was a hell of a fuck.

"Hippie?" She blinked big blues at me.

I craned my head back, annoyed at the ignorance. After righting my neck, I blew out a breath. "Bloome. Come on, now. Really? Flowers and shit?"

As I watched the red stain creep up her neck and into her face, she finally calmed and said, "My mother was told she couldn't have children. When she felt me blossoming in her womb, she called me Bloome. You got a problem with that?"

I cleared my throat before responding. "Let's get back to the issue at hand." I inclined my head at Viper. "We're here to keep the peace."

She looked angry and it just made me want to tear her clothes off faster. "And we're here to tell you that we do what want."

"And that means… what?" Phoenix asked.

The male witch—warlock—responded, the wine glass at his lips. "It means exactly what it means."

Phoenix addressed him. "Still not an explanation, man."

Bloome smacked her pale, freckled hand onto the table. "We don't answer to frickin' vampires."

"And who do you answer to?" I asked, staring into her eyes.

"Ourselves," an older woman responded. "I'm Iliana, I'm the council-slash-coven leader."

Viper sat forward in his seat. "Is that so? So you are a law unto yourselves?"

"Damn right we are," Bloome quickly replied, staring at me defiantly.

I huffed, annoyed. I looked at Iliana. "Good to know. However, you need to start policing your own."

Bloome narrowed her blue eyes at me. "What does that mean?"

Grinding my jaw, I replied, "It means that you need to put a fuckin' leash on bitches like Amara. She was killing humans."

"We weren't aware she was killing them," Iliana responded.

"Well, it's not okay," Viper responded.

The male witch waved a hand. "So what? There are billions on the planet."

I pounded my fist on the table and ignored the looks from my club brothers. "It doesn't matter, you asshole. You can't just go killing them for no reason. That's the reason for this meeting. We need to set some goddamn ground rules."

"We have our own rules," Bloome replied.

I looked at her square in her perfectly beautiful face and said, "It's clear that killing and assaulting humans are part of your 'rules' and that doesn't fly with us." I put up air quotes around the word *rules*.

"We've never answered to vampires and we never will. I'm not even sure why you called this meeting. You guys kill people, too. Don't try to deny it." Bloome smirked at me.

"Have you spoken to any wolves lately?" Face asked, staring at the group of witches.

"None of your business," Iliana replied.

Viper smacked a hand on the tabletop and said, "Maybe you should. Witches, vampires, and whatever else is out there. We don't put up with shit. We need to coexist with the humans… there's six billion of them on the fuckin' planet and we'll have no part of you exposing us or killing them. You dig?"

The witches all whipped their attention to my friend, and I resisted the urge to smile with pride.

"We're the closest thing to humans you'll find in the supernatural world," the male witch replied, looking bored as he gazed as his fingernails and rolled his eyes.

Before he could blink, I launched myself at him and used my talents to push him up against the wall of the bar. His face was two inches from the dartboard, which still had several darts imbedded in one of the boards.

I yanked out a dart and hovered it centimeters from his eyeball. He squeaked like a little bitch and squirmed.

"Listen here, and listen good. You may be close to humans, but you're not. I've seen the havoc you can wreak, and you'll not be doing that in New Orleans. Keep your spells and shit to yourselves. Oh, and if you think you can hex me or curse me or whatever you assholes do, you cannot. We've already put our own protections in place." I dropped him, and he fell to the floor.

A scream had us turning around. Bloome stood with her arms out, but no magic dripping.

"Magic doesn't work in here, sweetheart," I said, smiling.

"You're such an asshole!" the warlock snapped, gripping his neck. "Also, that beard of yours is just disgusting. Along with all other vampires. He scrabbled to his feet before making his way to the group of witches at the table.

I slowly made my way to the table. The look Viper gave me was hard to decipher. It was like he wanted to kill me, but he was proud of me, as well.

"It's time to go," I said, my adrenaline pumping. "We aren't changing our stance on this issue. Get in line with the rules or get the fuck outta New Orleans. It's really quite simple."

The witches got up and moved toward the front door of the Cobalt Room. Last to leave was Bloome. She turned around glared at me, her icy blue eyes boring into mine. I felt a small thrill rush through me when I realized she hadn't looked at anyone but me.

That thrill was short-lived, unfortunately. Through gritted teeth, she said, "We'll adhere. For now. But later on, you'll be wondering what messes you're cleaning up and who caused them, and there'll be no way you'll figure it out."

"Cute, sweetheart. Real cute," I replied, laughing.

7

WE BUILT THIS CITY

Bloome

These assholes. Who did they think they were? We'd been in this city for two centuries. Without so much as a peep from vampires, except the occasional attack when one would think we were unsuspecting humans. Now these jerks want to come into my city—*our* city—and tell us what to do?

Well, fuck that and fuck them.

No, what Amara did wasn't right. She wasn't in our coven and we'd looked the other way at the crap she was doing. It was *her* coven's responsibility to button her up and set her straight. But there was no way I was telling that neanderthal with the beard that. He and his leech friends weren't going to be privy to all the covens in the area. I could handle him just fine.

"How come our magic didn't work in there?" Brantley asked me.

I looked at him. He was a young, new warlock who had been raised in foster homes and had no idea what he was until we caught him doing clumsy magic one day. He was super bad at it, too. We took him into the coven about six months ago and taught him proper magic.

"They must have paid a witch to put a blocking spell around their club. I could feel the negative magic when I walked in. I tried to blast him off you, but it didn't work. I didn't figure it would, but I had to try."

He bumped his hip against mine and said, "Thanks, girl. I know you tried."

The walk back to our house was only a few blocks. I'd given Shadow a hard time earlier about giving me thirty minutes to have us ready, but it wasn't hard. I just liked ruffling his feathers because he was such a dick.

A dick I wish was uglier and nicer because he was neither of those things. I hated to admit my attraction to him. It infuriated me. I was taught my whole life to avoid vampires. They were soulless and unfeeling. Had no regard for human life or the rules. They were physically strong, and we were no match for them in that way. But it seemed all those things were contradicted by the way Shadow and his biker club friends behaved. Yes, I was sure they were stronger, but they didn't seem soulless or unemotional. And they seemed to care about humans more than the average vampire. I was going to have to do a little digging into these Nighthawks. I hadn't heard of them before they'd shown up in town a few months ago.

Still, we weren't going to be told what to do. I would admittedly be keeping a closer eye on some of the sketchier witches in town, just to keep these vampire vigilantes off our case and out of our business.

Skyla used her key to open the front door. "I'm gonna go take a bath. I feel gross after being around all those nasty vamps." She dramatically shuddered for effect, her blonde ringlets bouncing.

I laughed with a wave. "Knock yourself out."

I glanced around the house and closed my eyes to ensure everything was still in balance. I felt no strange magic, nor did I detect any sort of intruder or stranger had been inside during our absence.

The house was over one-hundred years old, and we'd worked hard to keep the original Victorian look to it, while modernizing the bathrooms and kitchen to make things easier on us. Boiling things in a big cauldron over a fire was the way of witches from a century ago. Ain't nobody got the energy for that type of time-suck anymore.

Six of us lived here, and we each had our own rooms. Our coven consisted of twenty witches, all females except Brantley. Some had families and lived on their own. Others just chose to live elsewhere. We held monthly coven meetings, and tomorrow, during the last night of the blood moon, we would hold our next one.

I went into my room and set my small purse on the bed. After peeling out of my black leather pants and red crop tank, I stood in front of my standing beveled mirror and gazed at my body. *Too fat,* I thought. My ass was a bit too big for my liking and my stomach could be flatter. I pulled at the fat on my hips and wished they were smaller. At least I liked my boobs. They could fill out a bra nicely but weren't so huge to where people made comments. Poor Skyla used baggy clothes to cover up her triple Ds and I wondered why she didn't just go have them surgically—or magically—reduced.

Sighing at the mirror, I frowned. I was only twenty-six... why was I putting on weight? I tried to watch what I ate but no amount of magic could keep me from the curse of aging or reverse my love for burritos and chocolate.

"*Illusio,*" I said, waving my hand while colorful sparks of magic floated from my fingertips.

In the mirror was now the woman wearing the body I wished I had. Tiny waist, slim but rounded hips, slender thighs. Cute bubble butt without a lot of jiggle. Sighing, I waved my hand again and it went back to the regular me.

"This is why I can't get a guy," I snapped at my reflection. "Then hit the gym, you lazy bitch," I countered.

Great. Now I'm talking to myself.

I gazed at my deathly pale skin in contrast to the black bra I wore. Admittedly, we witches kept to a night schedule. The sun empowered us as we slept, but the moon gave us the real power we craved. I'd been raised by witches and knew every spell and trick in the book, but it was the night that made me feel alive and powerful.

It reminded me of vampires. They couldn't go out into the sun and kept to the night schedule, just like us.

Vampires…

Like Shadow. That arrogant dick. Watching myself in the mirror, I reached up and touched my full bottom lip where he'd kissed me last night. Why had he done that?

"It was the only way to shut you up," he'd said.

Rude. I didn't need shutting up.

When I'd slapped him, I knew it wouldn't hurt him, but I couldn't let him get away with kissing me without my permission—even if I did find it hot. I found myself wishing he would do it again, and that really angered me.

Me… kissing a vampire. *As if!* Me… fucking a vampire… I wondered how big his cock was. He sure acted like he knew how to use it. I grew annoyed when my nipples pebbled in response to a mere thought about having sex with him. That broad chest, that deep, throaty voice. That beard and those full lips. Great, now my panties seemed to be getting warm and damp. *Dammit!* I blew out a breath and shook my head.

"Stop it, Bloome. You're not going to sleep with this guy. This vampire. He's dangerous and also a big, raging asshole!"

Still talking to myself… I'm surely going mad.

"Get a grip," I snapped at my reflection.

Putting my sexual thoughts away, I began to wonder how old he was. I knew those vamps never aged, which was also such a mystery to me. How was that possible? Magic?

I stripped out of my underwear and bra and threw on a tank and some pajama bottoms. After tossing my hair into a claw clip at the back of my head, I wandered downstairs into the library.

After flipping on the light, I wandered over to the right side of the bookshelves. "V… vampires."

I pulled out a large book with *Vampiric History* written on the side. I blew off the dust and went to sit on the small, covered bench that sat under a huge picture window. Glancing outside, I could see the street was quiet, the almost full moon glaring bright to illuminate the street.

With my back against the wall of the cove, I pulled my knees up to my chest and set the book against them. I began reading.

The usual lore about Vlad the Impaler came up, and I turned the pages. I'd read the books and seen the movies on Hollywood's take about vampire beginnings. This book I held, though, was three hundred years old. I had to be careful with the crispy, yellowed pages.

Something caught my eye. "…cursed to walk the earth, not aging or able to die," I read aloud. Wow, that sounded terrible. Why did vampires continue to make more vampires then? Wasn't that an awful existence?

But those Nighthawks vampires didn't seem miserable. Maybe they liked never growing old or dying. Me, personally… this world was so full of evil and fucked-up people, I was happy to do my eighty or ninety years and move on to the next life.

I continued to read aloud. "Lilith, first daughter of God and first witch, knowing Judas Iscariot had betrayed the Son of God, told him any offspring he created would also be cursed in the same way."

I put my finger on the passage and stared out the window into the night sky. "Harsh."

The moon reminded me of werewolves, and I vowed to pull that book next. Who else had pissed off an ancient witch and had been cursed to live as bloodthirsty animals once a month?

"Strength and rapid healing will compensate for the curse of never dying, keeping the man alive and impervious to aging, diseases, and plagues." I chuckled. "Of course. If a worldwide pandemic comes around again, these fuckers are gonna survive it." I shook my head.

In all honesty, we would too, as we had very powerful healing spells and herbs to keep us from getting sick. I'd heard of flus and colds but had never experienced them myself, as my mother had always kept us healthy with her spells and herbs. In fact, I'd never even been under the care of a human doctor in my life.

I flipped back to the beginning and read the table of contents until I found the section I was looking for: *How to kill a vampire.*

Running my finger down the page, I stopped when I came to the part I was looking for. "No creature can live without its head, so that is obvious. Keep your blades as sharp as possible. Removing the head is the easiest way to end a vampire. A stake of any material into the heart will also cause it to turn to ash and die. Any other method of killing, such as poison, smothering, arrows, or extreme blood loss will not kill the creature. You must destroy the brain or heart."

Interesting. Not that I was too surprised by the facts.

Could I kill Shadow and his friends? Yes, yes, I could. Would I be able to do it while Shadow looked at me with those strange gray eyes while I did it? I wasn't sure. All I knew was that our lives here in New Orleans had been perfectly content until these bossy and intrusive vampires had come to town, and there was no way I was going to sit back and let them tell me or my coven what to do.

8

REVERSE A CURSE

Shadow

She looked up at me with frightened eyes. "I don't understand the question."

Phoenix glanced at me nervously and then said, "I'm sorry, ma'am. My partner can be pretty blunt. The question is—what happened after the wolf attacked you?"

She shook her head, glancing at me and then to Phoenix, who hooked a finger into the tie at his throat and pulled. The dude was older than dirt and didn't have much patience for our undercover cop attire.

"I don't know." The older woman bit down on her lip and looked down at her hands folded over the hospital bed covers. "It lunged at me, and I screamed. After it knocked me down, I just kept screaming and trying to push and kick it off me. But it still got me." She reached up and touched the bandage at her throat.

"I'm sorry," Phoenix said, "but the doctors say you'll be all right. Just need some time to heal. After the wolf bit you, did it do anything else? Like run off?"

She looked down and I could tell she was trying to recall what happened. She put her shaky hand back on her lap and said, "I'm sorry. I don't know. It happened so fast that all I remember is the wolf biting me and then I woke up here."

Fuck.

Typical human memory. Trauma tended to cause the brain to block out the really bad things. Made me wonder what was worse than getting your neck chomped on by a wolf that would cause you to not want to remember the rest.

"Well, thank you for your time, Mrs. Jameson. We'll be in touch if we have any more questions," Phoenix said, putting on a charming smile for the older woman.

We left the hospital and hopped on our bikes. Before starting mine up, I looked at my club brother. "I think we're gonna get nowhere with this one. No way to find the wolves who did it."

He nodded, his red hair shiny under the streetlamps from the parking lot of the hospital. "We're gonna have to get Venom to sniff them out, unfortunately."

I knew he was right. I simply nodded and started up my bike. We drove back to the clubhouse and I dreaded telling Viper that we had nothing. I didn't even think Venom could sniff them out, as the victim had been washed and carried no wolf scent on her whatsoever. Trust me, I'd also sniffed her out good.

"But weren't there two victims?" Viper asked, leaned back in his chair as he sat in front of the computer in his office.

"Yeah, but the other one died," I said, trying to rein in my anger at the thought. "The lady's husband. Succumbed to his injuries."

Viper's jaw ticked in annoyance. "Well, that's murder. So, we need to find this mutt."

"Agreed," Phoenix said, pulling the tie off over his head and balling it up in his fist. I bit back a smile at the way the dress shirt barely fit around his arms. The guy was yoked and was a gym junkie. I liked working out, too, but I never really noticed if it made a difference in my physique. I'd been the same size since I was turned all those years ago.

"After this blasted blood moon is over, and the full moon in general, we'll get with Venom and see if he can't sniff this wolf out. If we could even narrow it down to his pack, we'll get with the pack leader and make sure he knows he needs to discipline this wolf or give us the green light to do it."

We turned our heads when we saw Venom leave his cell and stop short before reaching us. The look in his eyes was both desperate and a little angry.

"Until you learn some kind of wolf sign language, I don't know why you bother coming over here, all pissed off at us," I said, my arms folded as I stared down at the wolf.

He narrowed his eyes at me. Such a human thing to do.

I let out a brief chuckle. "We'll discuss this tomorrow. I'll stay up and not go to sleep once the sun comes up. Deal?" I asked.

He nodded his head with a soft woof and turned tail, heading back toward his cell that we left unlocked.

"That has to be seriously frustrating," Face said, shaking his head.

"I agree, but what can we do?" Viper asked, staring at the wolf, who looked sad and almost defeated as he sat in his cage.

"I wish there was a way to prevent him from turning at all," Face said quietly, staring at the creature in contemplation.

I huffed. "It's a curse. Just like us." I pointed to myself then my brothers. "Not growing old, not dying. Confined by the night. At least his curse is only three days a month."

"A curse by a fuckin' witch," Phoenix said, almost snarling. He hated witches and I had yet to figure out why. He was the oldest of all of us and had quite an extensive history. One day I would sit him down and ask him about it. He'd only been with the Nighthawks for about three years and kept mostly to himself, especially when it came to his past. Still, he was loyal to a fault, and was always there when anyone needed him. Plus, he had that uber-cool fire-wielding power. He was the best kind of brother to have.

I laid a hand on his shoulder. "You're right, man. Now, where could we find such a witch?"

He raised an eyebrow at me. "I think you know one."

I chuckled and put my hand down. "I do, but she's not doing us any fucking favors. She hates my guts, as far as I could tell. Maybe you could go pay the curly blonde a visit, she seemed sweet on you."

He made a face of disgust, and then he scowled. "How about no?"

"That's what I thought," I said, laughing.

"He has a point though," Face said, typing something into that iPad he seemed to have attached to his hand.

"About what?" Viper asked.

"Witches," Face quickly replied, looking up at us. "If a witch is responsible for cursing all men with the lycanthrope disease, then it'll take a witch to undo it."

"A very powerful one," Phoenix said.

"Where are we going to find one, not only powerful enough, but one willing to do it?" I asked, glancing at Venom, who was now standing in the cell, rapt attention on us.

"Do some digging," Viper said to Face. "We're in New Orleans, for God's sake. There has to be tons of them around. I have money and I know everyone has a price."

"On it, boss," he replied, looking down at the electronic tablet and walking toward the offices.

The talk of witches got me thinking about the redhead. She would rather die than help us out, I'd concluded. Still, I wondered what it would take for her to listen to me. I could hit her up and see if she'd like to entertain our proposition. I just didn't think she was powerful enough. After all, she wasn't able to break the warding on the club in order to try to blast me into submission earlier. Which got me thinking.

"Hey, Vane... what about the witch who warded this place? Is she powerful enough?" I pointed around the space and toward the club. Both had strong hexes against witchcraft, and would only allow witches inside, but weakened or muted their power once inside.

He shook his head. "Kovah's wife, the BSI agent… she had a witch who owed her a favor, and she passed the favor onto us. The witch was set to go to that island prison of theirs for infractions. Getting her to ward the place and make it stick got her out of it. Now she only has to be on some kind of supernatural parole, checking in once a month with them or some shit."

"Yeah, but do you think she's powerful enough to try to reverse a werewolf curse?"

He shook his head. "I doubt it. She seemed pissed off even having to do this for us. She probably hates every creature except witches. Judging by the way she snarled at me when she warded the place."

Yikes.

"They're all like that," Phoenix commented. "Hateful and bitchy. I say we try to find another way to help out Venom." He glanced at the wolf, who was now lying down again, his muzzle resting on his front paws as he took in our conversation.

"I agree," I said, thinking of Bloome. She seemed cranky and wanted nothing to do with us, so I could see where Phoenix was coming from. He obviously had his own history with witches or probably a single witch—that seemed more likely the more I got to know the cat. He was cool but could hold a serious fucking grudge.

I watched as Face disappeared into the hallway that led to the offices and hoped he'd be able to come up with something—not that I was holding my breath. Wolves had been around for centuries and I'd personally had my own run-ins with them, having almost been turned into one myself a very long time ago.

3

RUDELY INTERRUPTED

Bay City, Michigan – 1954

I spent three years working at the hotel and living with Alfie. It had worked out nicely, and by being frugal, I was able to save up a lot of money so I could get a place of my own. After I got a job at the local factory in town, I made even more money and was able to sock most of it away, even after I got my own place, a small studio apartment in a building converted from a hotel into apartments.

I met a nice young lady named Saundra and we began dating seriously. After about six months, I felt like it was time for me to think about proposing. I was twenty and she was nineteen, still living with her folks on the outskirts of town. I had kept in contact with my parents but didn't see them very often, just on holidays and recently for my mom's fiftieth birthday party a few months prior.

Believe it or not, going into the woods was one of my favorite things to do. It helped me clear my head and the quiet forest sounds helped soothe me. I had never brought Saundra there, but the following Saturday, I decided we'd go have a picnic together so we could talk. I wanted to propose but needed to get a feel as to where she was at with it all. I had my eye on a ring at a shop in town but had yet to buy it. I guessed I was just a little gun-shy about it all.

I parked my new-to-me 1941 Chevrolet Coupe Pickup on a side street and killed the engine. After opening Saundra's door and helping her out of the vehicle, I grabbed the picnic basket I'd packed earlier and led her toward the thicket of trees. Hand-in-hand, we walked deeper into the forest until I found a clearing. I removed the blanket from the basket and spread it on the ground before helping her sit.

She looked around, her dark-brown hair shining under the beams of sun escaping through the gaps in the trees above us.

She looked straight into my eyes. "This is a strange place to have a picnic." She seemed as if she was forcing a smile. "I think the park in town would have sufficed." She reached up and placed a soft, warm hand on my cheek. "Don't you, Craig?"

"Yes, I do. But I like to come here sometimes to clear my head. It's quiet and I wanted to be alone with you. Are you uncomfortable? We can leave…"

"No," she replied quickly, still smiling. "I like it just fine here. It's just… different."

I pulled out two ham and cheese sandwiches and two glass bottles of milk. I handed her one of each and began to unwrap my sandwich.

"I'm so hungry," she replied, unwrapping hers. She took a bite and smiled at me. "This is really good."

"Tom at Happy Belly Deli made it. I think they use some secret sauce or something to make it taste extra delicious," I replied, smiling because I was glad she loved it.

After taking a swig of milk, she set the bottle down and said, "Craig, I have something to tell you."

I set my sandwich down and grabbed her hand, staring into her caramel-colored eyes. "What is it, sweetie?"

Saundra took a deep breath and looked at our linked hands. "I've been trying to find a way to tell you this… but I can't think of any way to make it easier, so I'll just come out with it."

Ugh. My stomach was in knots now, the ham and cheese feeling like it might come back up. "Spill the beans, please."

She looked up at me and said, "I have to leave Bay City. My family and I are moving to Ohio. Dad got a job managing a huge automotive factory out there. It's a big promotion for him. We leave in two weeks."

I felt like I'd been punched in the gut. "But you're nineteen. You are an adult. You can stay here, can't you?"

She shook her head, her face downcast. "Daddy says it's not proper for a woman my age to live alone. Not to mention, I don't think I can afford my own place working at the ice cream shoppe."

Well, there was an easy solution for that. I pulled her into my lap and brushed some hair from her face. "Listen, doll. I was going to ask your dad first, but I guess I'll just bring it up now. I was planning on proposing."

She gasped, her eyes wide. "You were?"

I nodded. "Yes, I was. And I will, so once that happens, I'm sure your pop will be okay with you staying here, since we'll be getting married. Right?"

She chewed her lip, her eyes glistening. "Yes, I think he will be."

"Is that what you want, though?" I asked her.

She nodded immediately. "Yes!"

I brought my lips to hers and kissed her softly. I slowly introduced tongue and she turned around and straddled me. As I hugged her to me, the kiss became more passionate, more urgent. My dick was straining behind my zipper but obviously I would have to deal with him later. There was no way I was going to go all the way for the first time with her right here and now.

Panting, she pulled away and stared at me. "Wow. That was intense. I can't wait for our wedding night!"

"Hey, I haven't even proposed yet!" I joked.

She leaned down and kissed me again. "I'll give you a hint: I'm not gonna say no."

I laughed and we kissed once more before she reached down

and fed me the rest of my sandwich. We spent the rest of the day talking and taking walks through the trees.

I breathed a sigh of relief when I got into my car. After starting it up and driving away from Saundra's house, I couldn't wipe the smile from my face. Her father had given his blessing for me to propose, and I was so glad I'd already bought the ring because showing it to him and her mom seemed to earn me extra brownie points with them.

After parking the car in front of the ice cream shop, I whistled as I went inside. I sat at the counter, grinning as Saundra had her backside to me from where she was making a milkshake with a machine. Her derriere looked very nice in that short skirt.

"What's a guy gotta do to get some service around here?" I asked playfully.

She turned around, a practiced smile on her face, although I could tell she looked a little miffed, and then relaxed when she saw me. "Oh, it's you. Don't you know you're my favorite customer? What can I get ya, handsome?"

"Just a mint chocolate chip cone, double scoop, please."

"You got it." She winked at me.

I heard a scoffing noise and turned to see an older lady eating an ice cream sundae staring at Saundra. She shook her head. "Flirting like that in public. For shame." She looked at the man seated across the table from her, presumably her husband, and said, "I would have never been so blatant and bold like that at her age."

"Yes, I know, Joyce," the man replied dryly, sounding exasperated.

I bit back a smile and shook my head. I loved it when Saundra winked at me and called me 'handsome.'

We made small talk while I ate my cone and she worked, then I got up to leave. "I'll pick you up at six sharp," I said, leaving fifty cents on the counter.

"Your cone was only ten cents, silly," she replied.

"Keep it." I winked at her.

"See you tonight," she replied, shoving the extra coins in her apron pocket.

I had two hours to kill so I went to the big and tall department store and got myself a new shirt and some aftershave for the special night. Then, after getting ready, I got into my car and went to pick up Saundra.

I was so nervous but knew I needn't be. She was going to say yes and that was all there was to it. It had been two weeks since our forest picnic, and every time we spent time alone, she always looked at me with hope and anticipation, but I purposely kept her waiting until the last minute. Her family was moving in a week and I knew time was running out.

After a fancy steak dinner, we drove to the bay, and as we got out, I was suddenly very nervous. The ring box was burning a hole in my pocket.

We walked along the beach, hand in hand, the summer night breeze perfect. She stopped to look out over the water, the full moon shining down on the small waves as we looked at the city lights across the bay.

With her back to my front, I wrapped my arms around her, and we stood like that for several minutes. Then, I turned her around and looked down into her face. I had sprouted up in inches over the past couple years, it seemed, so she had to really crane her neck up to look at me.

"I love you Saundra Fischer." I got down on one knee, pulling the ring box from my pocket at the same time and presenting it to her on the flat of my palm. "Will you marry me?"

She nodded immediately and screamed, "Yes!"

I slid the ring on, and she beamed at it. "It's beautiful!"

I lifted her in a hug and spun her around as we kissed.

Once I set her down, I bent down to kiss her again, but stopped short when I heard a threatening growl come from behind me. I slowly turned around to see what looked like a large gray wolf standing there, teeth bared, drool dribbling from its jaws.

Saundra let out a bloodcurdling scream that pierced the quiet night.

10

LET'S MAKE A DEAL

Shadow

The bright lights of the diner made her hair glow extra bright red. I'd never seen hair that shiny before.

"What? Do I have something in my hair?" Bloome asked, reaching up and running her fingers through it.

I cleared my throat. "No."

"Then why are you staring at it?" she asked, setting her menu down.

Because I want to grab it in my fist and yank your head back while I fuck you from behind.

At my lack of response, she shook her head and looked down at the menu. "You're weird."

"Are you ready to order?" the server asked as she appeared at our table.

"Cobb salad, side of ranch," she replied.

The young lady then looked at me. "You, sir?"

"You serve liquor?" I asked, running my fingertips over my beard.

"Yes, what can I get you?"

"Just a bourbon, neat, honey," I replied.

She wrote it down and said, "No food?"

"No, I ate earlier," I replied.

After the woman walked off with our orders, I looked at Bloome.

She made a face. "I bet you did."

Chuckling, I said, "I did. Blood is food. I didn't lie."

"Gross," she replied with an exaggerated gag noise.

"Like you guys don't use blood in your spells. Don't act like it grosses you out, sweetheart."

She lifted her chin. "We don't ingest it."

"Tomato, tomahto."

She sighed dramatically, then folded her hands together before placing them on the checkered tabletop of the old-fashioned diner. "What do you want, Shadow?"

"You can call me Craig. But only because I like you," I said, throwing her my most charming smile.

Her eyes bounced to my cut and nametag, then back to me. "Such an ordinary name for guy like you."

I chuckled. "Well, thanks. I think."

She shifted in her booth seat, stretching a long, pale thin arm along its length while staring at me. "I had pegged you as a Joe or a Thor."

"Well, Craig was quite the fashionable Irish name in 1931 when I was born." I tiled my head and smirked at her. "I'm sure my parents set a trend with it."

Her eyes went wide, and she almost choked on her water before setting it down. "Nineteen… what?"

I laughed again, offering her my napkin to wipe the water dribble all over her chin. "I said what I said."

"Fuck, you're old," she said, taking the proffered napkin and cleaning up the water.

"I'm aware," I said, still grinning at her reaction. "How old are you, anyway?"

She set the glass down and stared at me for a few uncomfortable seconds. "Twenty-six."

"Well, you're older than me, then." I winked at her.

She furrowed her brow, those reddish eyebrows dipping together. "How do you figure?"

"Your bourbon. Neat," the server said, setting down the glass. She looked at Bloome. "Food's almost out."

I thanked her then ran my fingertip around the rim of the glass. "I was turned at twenty-four. So… that makes you older than me." I was well aware these were irrelevant details, I just wanted to mess with her. She seemed to get riled easily, and ruffling Bloome's feathers seemed to become a new favorite hobby of mine.

I'm such a dick…

"You're as old as dirt. So, I'll just call you 'old man' from now on. How's that?"

I lifted a shoulder and let it fall. "Fine by me, red."

"That's not something you're going to keep calling me, dude. Seriously stop it." She set her jaw and sat back in the booth with her arms folded across her chest. A very nice chest, I might add.

My eyes drifted down to the black half-shirt she wore, showing the swell of her tits, her smooth, pale stomach, and cute bellybutton her jeans almost hid. I licked my lips and looked up into her impossible blue eyes.

"But you're so cute when you're angry," I supplied.

"I'm not angry," she countered, narrowing her eyes at me, that V between her eyebrows belying her words.

"I call bullshit," I said, picking up my bourbon and shooting it back in one shot. It burned going down my throat and I sighed in contentment. I just wished I could get catch a buzz at least from one drink. *Ah, the good old days…*

"Bullshit about what?" she asked.

The server set her salad and dressing in front of her. "Anything else, ma'am?"

Bloome shook her head. "No, thank you, Tracy, I'm good."

I just now noticed the server's nametag and felt like an ass for not addressing her by name earlier. I had become too accustomed to dismissing humans anymore. I supposed I shouldn't do that and vowed to do better.

I watched Tracy walk off and then said, "You are pissed. Your eyes get this stormy look, and then your forehead wrinkles and your lips set together firmly when you're mad."

The forkful of salad paused at her lips, and she dipped those brows again, seemingly in question. "You don't miss a detail, do you?"

I shook my head and plucked a toothpick from the container set on the table. I twirled it between my fingers before saying, "No, sweetheart, I do not."

She shoveled the vegetables into her mouth and stared at me as she chewed. There was defiance and amusement dancing in her gaze, and I felt my dick rise to attention. Why was her sass turning me on?

After swallowing, she said, "What do you want, Craig?"

"I need your help," I replied before placing the toothpick between my teeth.

"With what?" she asked, drizzling the last of the dressing onto her salad and then mixing it around.

"How powerful are you?" I asked.

She looked up from her stirring, the fork frozen in place. "I'm a lesser witch if that's what you're asking. I'll be a greater witch in about four years."

My chewing of the toothpick stopped. "The fuck does that mean?"

She shook her head with a laugh. "It means I have powers, and know spells, but I'm limited."

"I see," I replied, nodding. "So, you can't undo a werewolf curse?"

She started coughing and almost choked, the salad threatening to expel itself out of her mouth. She swallowed what I assumed was a bite that wasn't ready to be swallowed, and then replied, "No. *Hell* no."

The half-shirt she wore was some sort of tank top and I looked in amusement as a cubed tomato fell right into the crack of her cleavage. A stray lettuce leaf sat on the swell of her right boob and I pointed at it. "Need help with that?"

Bloome glanced down and quickly swiped up the food, dropping it into her salad bowl. For the first time, I saw a blush steal across her pale, freckled cheeks. "No. No thanks."

"Well, do you know any witches who are powerful enough to undo a werewolf curse?" I asked, staring into her light eyes to avoid looking at her tits again. I was hoping I'd get to see them free and bared for me at some point.

She set her fork down and placed her hands in her lap. "Why?"

"Not your concern. Just asking," I replied.

She shook her head. "Not my concern... it sure as hell *is* my concern. Why would you want to undo a werewolf's curse? I thought y'all were natural enemies and all that jazz."

Yep... she was right. How would I explain this one?

I blew out a breath and rubbed my hand over my beard before folding my hands on the tabletop. "We are. It's just that we actually have this ally wolf... well, he's more of a friend... and he's a Nighthawk. So, we'd like him to—"

She cut me off, her hand in the air. "Wait, wait, wait." She grinned, shaking her head. "So, you have a *werewolf* in your *vampire* biker club? How the hell did that happen?" she asked, looking very amused.

I had always prided myself on being tight-lipped and today I was kicking myself. What was it about this witch that had me thinking about the *loose lips sinking ships* adage?

"Yes, we do. It's a long story, and not mine to tell and all that," I defended. "Bottom line—I hate wolves and wish for my friend to just be a human. Or a vampire if he chooses."

"Why do you hate wolves? I mean, I guess if it's a natural enemies thing like you said—"

"It's not that," I snapped. Then I calmed down. "I'm sorry. Well, can you?"

She shook her head. "Okaaaay. Well, regardless, if he's natural born, there's not a damn thing we can do about it."

Disappointment flooded me. I wanted to bring back good news to Viper, and more importantly, Venom. "Understandable. But do you have any idea how the werewolf first came about?"

She nodded. "It's pretty simple and a little cliché, to be honest." She smiled despite the conversation and looked down into her half-eaten salad. "A woman burned by a guy."

I'd read something similar but wanted a witch's take on it.

"Go on, red," I said.

She narrowed her eyes at me but didn't correct me. "Our lore tells us that a witch named Althea was in complete and utter love with a man named Mathias. He was good to her until he wasn't. When he cheated on her, she went berserk. Sold her very soul to the devil to create a spell that would curse Mathias to turn into a feral beast at every full moon."

"Wow, a woman scorned takes on a new meaning," I joked.

Bloome grinned. "You're exactly right. Althea was pissed."

"But why a wolf?" I asked, genuinely curious.

She shrugged one pale shoulder. "Apparently, a wolf howled in the distance as she was performing the spell and that was the animal she chose. To top it off, all women who fell in love with these creatures and became impregnated would give birth to wolves as well. Even if they were human."

"Harsh," I replied, suppressing a shudder. But… at least they could reproduce. I'd have to turn someone—an adult—to have some semblance of an offspring, and there was no fucking way I'd do that.

"Very," Bloome replied. She tossed her wadded up paper napkin into the mostly eaten salad and sat back. "Is that what you wanted to ask me?"

The server brought the bill and set it on the tabletop. I snatched it up and plunked my card on top before Bloome could even blink.

"But you didn't even eat," she argued, pointing at the bill.

I shrugged. "Yeah, but that bourbon wasn't cheap."

She stared hard at me, her eyes reflecting something between curiosity and lust. "Is that all you asked me here for?"

"For the most part," I replied, twirling the toothpick between my fingers as I refused to break eye contact with the beautiful, sassy witch.

"Okay… what does that mean?" she asked, matching my stare.

I paused, knowing I should take the slow approach but also wanting to get a rise out of her. "It means I also asked you here because I want to fuck you and hear you scream my name as I make you come. But if you're not down for some skin on skin, or mouth on pussy, we could do some other shit, like go play mini golf."

Blue eyes wide, she gasped, and I watched in amusement as she quickly recovered with a sassy smirk. Sucking in a deep breath, she said, "Let's try mini golf first. If you're not a total prick during, and you don't cheat at the game, then maybe we'll fuck. Deal?"

I grinned and tossed the used toothpick into her dirty salad plate before it was whisked away by Tracy. "Definitely a deal."

11

FIGHTING ATTRACTION (AND LOSING)

Bloome

My heart was slamming in my chest as I sprinted down the sidewalk and toward my house. I had never—and I mean never—had a guy that upfront and blunt in my life. My underwear was soaked at his direct approach and dirty talk, and I couldn't figure out why that was turning me on so much.

It didn't help matters that as we had left the diner, he'd wrapped me in his arms and kissed me silly. He was huge—not sure how tall but I'd never met anyone as tall as him—and when his big, hard arms wrapped around my backside and pulled me flush against him, I'd turned into a helpless pile of goo, as pliable as the Play-Doh I'd played with in kindergarten all those years ago.

Why that made me both angry and thrilled at the same time, I couldn't explain. I was a strong, independent witch and didn't need some man—certainly some vampire—making me feel all mushy and vulnerable after one damn dinner. And here I was, agreeing to another date that could possibly end in sweaty, mind-blowing sex.

But really… what had happened last time I'd agreed to a date that could possibly end up in sex? I was burned. The guy—Mick—he'd been funny and charming at dinner and the movie we went to, but at the end of the date, I'd foolishly—after too many glasses of wine—agreed to go back to his place. Well, let's just say, Mick had been a five-pump chump with a small dick and had fallen asleep before I had even known what had happened.

Craig—Shadow—whatever, he didn't seem that way. There was a cocky swagger about him, not to mention his size, that told me he was different. My dad, he was a tall guy, about six-foot-four. Craig was taller than him. I'd never measured my attraction to a guy based on height, but the safety and warmth I'd felt after that kiss and the way his arms and big hands had made me felt protected... I couldn't help but realize what all the fuss was about.

There was no way he had a tiny dick and didn't know how to use it—right? He was how old? He'd said he was born in 1931. That made him, like, ninety. Surely, he'd fucked plenty of women and knew how to please them.

I put the key into the door to my old Victorian house and then turned the lock to secure it behind me. The house was quiet, and for that I was grateful.

The salad at that diner had been good, but for some reason, I was still hungry. I wandered into the kitchen and opened the fridge. I grabbed the container of eggs and pulled out two, setting them on the countertop. I quickly scrambled them with some milk and salt and pepper and before tossing the mixture into a glass bowl. One minute in the microwave and I had a fast, hot snack which I gobbled down quickly.

After putting the bowl and fork into the dishwasher, I went up to my room and stripped out of the red leather pants and black crop top before wandering to the bathroom. Just as I was about to start up the shower, the doorbell chimed.

A quick glance at my phone showed almost midnight. Who the hell was ringing our doorbell this late?

I tossed on an oversized Twenty One Pilots concert tee and wandered downstairs. I found it odd none of my roommates had come to the door. A peek through the peephole showed Shadow—Craig—standing there.

What the! I never gave him my address. I slowly opened it. "What are you—"

My question was cut off by sexy lips assaulting mine. His beard tickled my chin, but I didn't care. I kissed him back. He lifted me up so I was straddling him, and oh, my God—that thick cock of his was pushing against my bare core, which was instantly damp—and I groaned into his mouth.

His hand reached up under my tee and twisted my nipple. I almost cried at how much that aroused me.

"Fuck mini golf. I need you now," he whispered into my ear.

"Up the stairs, first door on the left," was my breathy response before I slammed my lips back onto his.

He made it up the stairs in record time, and as soon as my back was on the mattress to my bed, I heard the ripping of my beloved concert tee being torn from my body.

"Hey! I liked that shirt!" I protested.

At his lack of response, I looked up to see him gazing lustily and appreciatively down at my body. My legs widened, and before I could blink, he lowered his head between them and stuck his tongue out. I watched with wide eyes as he shoved it into my wet hole, and then laved his way up my clit, never breaking eye contact.

I almost came and cried at the same time. "Oh, my God," I whimpered.

He did this several times, his beard tickling my ass and inner thighs. His big, rough hands gripped my legs, spreading them so wide it almost hurt. He took one hand and moved it to my sopping wet hole, shoving one finger inside and pumping it in and out.

"Fuck your pussy tastes so good," he moaned between licks and sucks of my clit.

My legs shook uncontrollably as a tsunami built in my lower belly and erupted out between my legs as he continued his delicious assault on my core. "Craig!" I screamed, bucking against his mouth and fingers.

"Oh, yes, baby. I feel that pussy clenching on my fingers. I hope you're ready for my cock now."

I was still riding my climax and about to come again at his filthy talk. "Fuck me, Craig. Please. Fuck me hard. Give it to me," I begged with a full-body shudder.

What the hell! I never talk like this!

My tits were standing at attention, my nipples pebbled and hard, wanting more of him.

Shadow licked his fingers as he stared at me. He pulled his shirt and cut off before kicking out of his boots and jeans—no underwear. *Hot.* Then positioned himself between my legs, up on his knees. He rubbed a thick finger over my wet and greedy core before grabbing his cock and lining up the head with my needy hole.

I looked down and gasped with wide eyes at the size. "Baby... I don't know if that will fit..."

He shoved a finger over my lips before leaning down and placing his mouth over mine.

I immediately relaxed, lost in his sensuous kiss and the way his mouth was calming me. His tongue mingled with mine, and when he reached down to roll his fingers over my pebbled nipple, I immediately arched my back into his chest, getting aroused again.

We kissed some more as I felt the head of his cock teasing my dripping wet entrance.

"You want me?" he asked quietly between kisses.

"Yes," I moaned in return.

He kissed me again, then said, "Say you want me to fuck you, Bloome."

"Fuck me. Please," I begged again. My hips inadvertently met his, and when his dick slid into me, I whimpered into his mouth.

Holy huge cock... that stretch was something between pleasure and pain. But I took it like a champ, rewarded when his groan met my ear.

He moved at a torturously slow pace, now up on his hands staring at me. "Are you okay?"

It had hurt for just a second, but now I wanted more. I gripped his massive shoulders and aggressively shoved my hips up to meet his. "Yes. Fuck me hard. Please, baby."

His features relaxed, and then he began to move harder and faster, sliding himself in and out of me while not breaking eye contact. It was the hottest thing I had ever experienced. The feel of his thick member sliding over my sensitive bundle of nerves and then assaulting my g-spot had me shivering.

When he leaned down and pulled one of my puckered nipples into his mouth, I raised my hips, chasing that second orgasm. It wasn't long until I found it, him whispering in my ear that he was close and about come. I shivered hard when the climax erupted through my body at the same time he stilled, shooting his load into me, his dick throbbing as he pumped, and his breaths erratic and panting in my ear. I whimpered and bucked against him, my nipples hard and rubbing against his massively hard muscular chest.

Once he collapsed on me and then rolled over, I knew there was no going back for us.

What had I just done? I barely knew this guy—this *vampire*.

"Damn, that was amazing," Craig said, staring up at the ceiling with his hands behind his head. He slowly looked over at me for a response.

He was right but I was loath to admit it. Why? I wasn't sure.

"You don't agree?" he asked at my silence.

"I agree, it's just that we… uh, we moved pretty fast."

He leaned up on his elbow and ran his finger over my chest and up to my throat before stopping at my chin so he could turn it to look at him. "The laws of attraction are undeniable. I would think as a witch, you'd know that."

Defensively, I replied, "Yes, I do know that. But it's just lust."

He frowned. "Well, now I'm offended."

"You should be flattered," I replied dryly. "I don't just sleep with random dudes. I slept with you because you're sexy and hot."

He stared at me with those freakishly cool gray-silver eyes and said, "So sexy and hot, yes. But not relationship material."

Relationship material? I almost wanted to laugh but refrained. Was this guy serious? "Craig, I can't be in a relationship with anyone, period. Let alone a vampire."

"And what's so wrong with being with a vampire?" he asked, staring at me expectantly while running circles on my arm with this finger.

I looked down, rubbing my hand over his arm. "First off, you're only up at night, and—"

"So are witches," he interrupted.

"I know," I replied, frustrated. "Second, you need to stick to your own kind. So y'all can live forever together."

"I could turn you," he replied with a smile now.

I stared at him in horror. "Turn me? Absolutely not."

"You say that like it's a bad thing," he said.

Huffing, I replied, "It *is* a bad thing. Plus, I would turn into a succubus. No way."

He stared at me long and hard and then nodded. "You're right. I wouldn't wish this life on anyone, anyway."

I grinned. "One roll in the hay and you're ready to make me into your mate? You're crazy."

Immediately, he frowned. "Don't call me that."

"Okay then. Sorry about that." I wasn't sure why I was apologizing.

Shadow got up and began putting his clothes on.

"Leaving so soon?" I glanced at my bedside clock. It was only one a.m. We had hours before the sun came up.

He nodded, buttoning up his pants and reaching for his T-shirt. After pulling it over his head, he said, "Yeah, it's the right thing to do."

"I'd like you to stay," I said, now regretting my words.

He shrugged, shoving his feet into his boots. "It's all good, sweetheart. Maybe next time." He looked up at me. "If there is a next time."

Then, he disappeared into thin air like I'd seen him do before and cursed myself for not asking just how the hell he did that.

I swore, wishing I had a number other than the repair shop so I could tell him to get his fine, sexy ass the hell back here and cuddle with me, dammit.

12

STORIES & SCARS

Bay City, Michigan – 1951

What the hell was a wolf doing on the shores of the bay here in Bay City? Well, I thought it was a wolf, anyway. Maybe it was a coyote? I internally kicked myself for not being more savvy about the distinction.

"Craig?" Saundra whimpered as I shoved her behind me.

"Go! Scram!" I said to the creature, shooing it away with my hands as if it was just an annoying dog.

It growled again and I briefly glanced behind me to see where we could run in case it pounced. I swore when I saw we had nowhere to go, except into the bay. I could swim but I had never asked Saundra if she could.

As the wolf took several slow, threatening steps toward us, I looked around again and saw a couple walking hand-in-hand up the beach several yards away.

"Hey!" I yelled, waving my arms. "Hey!"

They stopped walking and just looked at me. "Call the dog catchers. Or the cops. There's a stray wolf or coyote here, but I think it's rabid and dangerous!"

The two turned around and ran toward the historical building where tourists could learn the history about the bay and the area.

"Craig..." she whimpered again and then she suddenly screamed when the creature lunged at us.

We turned and ran toward the water, but I quickly shifted us to run up the beach, where the couple was, and avoid the water. Running in sand felt like running in slow motion and the wolf was catching up to us quickly.

I pushed Saundra in front of me and told her to run. I wished I had my father's gun at this moment. I felt helpless and terrified that I couldn't protect my fiancée like I should be able to. I was strong, my muscles had gotten exponentially bigger from working on heavy machinery at the plant, and I was pretty tall now, but still… I didn't think my size would be a match against a wolf barehanded.

I looked behind me a split second before the creature pounced on my back, knocking me into the sand. I heard Saundra scream and I yelled at her to go get help before my face smashed into the cool sand. I yelled when I felt teeth dig into my neck and used all my might to try to buck the wolf off of me. Its growling and hot, rancid breath so close to my ear was something I will never, ever forget.

Finally, I managed to roll over and it let go of my neck. Bloody drool swung from its jaws as it tried to bite me again. I held him off with my long arms, his teeth still inches from my face. Suddenly, its paw came up and swiped at me. I turned my head and felt a burning pain above my left eye. Instantly, blood began to dribble down the side of my face.

"Hell no!" I snapped. Without thinking, I punched the creature in its snout several times and it shook its head as if dazed and backed off. I took the opportunity to stand up tall and back into the water. Something told me this creature wouldn't follow me there.

Once I was waist deep, I stood in the freezing cold water and watched the wolf seeming to stare at me from the shoreline. I said nothing; just stared back at it. The faint sounds of police sirens were getting louder and closer. The wolf turned its head toward the sounds and suddenly bolted away, through some trees, and disappeared into the night.

Still frozen with fear and with cold from the water, I forced myself to shore and sat down. I hoped Saundra was all right. The wolf hadn't hurt her, but she had to be scared out of her wits. As my adrenaline came down, I felt piercing pain on the back of my neck. I reached back with my wet hand and saw a lot of blood.

Then, I started feeling woozy. I placed my hands on the sand to try to steady myself, just as I heard screaming and yelling coming from up the shore. Through hazy eyes, I saw Saundra and two uniformed cops running toward me. My breaths left my body a little too quickly, and before they could reach me, my world was engulfed in darkness.

Blinking open eyelids that felt like they weighed a metric ton, I quickly closed them tight against my harsh, white environment. The smell of something strong and sterile hit my nose, and I wrinkled it. My neck and forehead burned and ached. I groaned.

"He's awake," I heard Saundra say excitedly.

Forcing my eyes open now, I saw my fiancée and a police officer standing next to my hospital bed. I tried to sit up, but a nurse quickly rushed over and fussed at me. "Go slow now," she said.

I did as she said, and once the pillows were fluffed behind me so I could sit comfortably, I reached up to touch my forehead. A big bandage was over my eyebrow and left side of my forehead. Reaching behind me, I felt a bigger one on my neck.

"How long have I been out?" I asked, still feeling dazed.

The nurse, whose nametag read Millie, scribbled something on a clipboard before looking at me. "Last night and all of today. Had to do surgery on you. Your wounds required quite a bit of cleaning from all the sand before the doctor could sew them up." She shook her head. "Doc Mullins said he'd never seen a gash quite that deep before." She used the pen to indicate my neck.

Saundra walked slowly toward me and gingerly wrapped her arms around my shoulders. After pulling back, she bit her lip and tears filled her eyes. "I'm so glad you're okay. I was so scared, Craig."

I lifted a hand and rubbed my thumb across her cheek. "I know, doll. I'm sorry."

"May I have a few minutes alone with him?" the police officer asked Saundra and the nurse.

"Of course," the nurse replied, practically dragging my fiancée out behind her. "Visiting hours are over, anyway."

"I'll be back tomorrow," Saundra called out before the door closed.

"Mr. Walsh, I'm Officer Elmwood with the Bay City Police. What can you tell me about last night?"

I thought back to everything from when we got out of the car, to my proposal, to the wolf. I told him all of it.

"Why did the wolf attack you, do you think?" Officer Elmwood asked.

"I have no idea. Why was there a wolf wandering around the beach anyway? It just sort of came out of nowhere."

The officer jotted down notes as I spoke and nodded. "I agree. It's a very strange case indeed."

"Hey, have there been any other wolf attacks around the area? I do read the newspaper, but I haven't been able to over the past few days."

He shook his head. "No."

"I'm no wolf expert, but is this normal behavior? Don't they usually attack when feeling threatened? I did nothing to the animal. And it was sort of bizarre the way it ran off when it heard sirens. Almost like it knew the cops were coming."

"You're correct," he replied. "That's why we're working hard to find it. It'll be put down immediately upon capture."

I nodded and sighed in relief. The quicker they found the beast, the better.

Officer Elmwood closed his notepad and said, "If you think of any other details, please come down to the station on Oak Street and ask for me."

"Of course," I replied.

Just then, a doctor and the same nurse walked in. The officer tipped his hat at them and left.

"Hi, Craig. I'm Doctor Mullins," he said. The man was probably in his sixties, chubby with red cheeks, and an easy smile. "Let's take a look."

The nurse handed him some kind of weird-looking scissors and he cut the bandages away from the back of my neck. "Healing nicely, stitches holding up beautifully." He pointed at my neck and the nurse began to re-bandage it. "Are you in much pain?"

I nodded. "Admittedly, yes, my neck and eyebrow hurt."

"Millie will get you some more morphine when she's done," he replied, now pulling the bandage away from my forehead. "This one is also looking nice, only required a couple of stitches." He stood back from me and said, "Unfortunately, the cut was pretty deep and the hair on your eyebrow there probably won't grow back. You'll have a scar. We've got some doctors who are learning about cosmetic stitching and scar revision, things like that, if you'd like me to put you in touch with them. They are students and need subjects."

I shook my head. Students? No thanks. "It's all right. I'm sure I can live with a little scar."

He chuckled and said, "And you'll have a neat-o story to tell about it, as well."

"You got that right," I said, more about the story and less about how "neat-o" it would be having to re-tell it over and over. As of now, I just wanted to get out of here and forget any of this ever happened.

13

MURDER AT ZOMBIES

Shadow

Face laughed at me. "You just hit it and quit it, huh?"

"It wasn't like that," I muttered, feeling vulnerable and actually quite stupid that I'd kissed and told. Why had I done that?

"Yes, it was," Kovah replied, lifting the beer to his mouth with a grin. "It's cool, though. She's hot. Just don't turn her." His face went serious and stormy.

I ignored the succubus-hater. "Well, she didn't want me there," I groused, downing the shot Dash had just poured me.

"If y'all are done gossiping like hens in here, we have a situation," Viper said, as he walked to our table inside the Cobalt Room.

Thankful for the reprieve of the ribbing I'd been getting from my brothers—one I would never admit I deserved—we got up and followed Viper out of the bar and into the main area of the warehouse—our clubhouse.

"More witch trouble," Viper started. He looked down at his phone and continued, "Theo reported three piles of ash behind his bar in the Quarter."

"Who's Theo?" Paz asked, coming out of the bike repair shop, wiping his hands on an oil rag. The prospect had proven to be very useful, and the kid seemed to have a good head on his shoulders.

He was getting patched soon and I could see him making lieutenant one day.

Viper turned to look at him. "Hey, Paz. Huddle up." He pointed to where he and we five lieutenants stood. Once Paz was in the circle, he continued, "Theo owns Zombies, a bar in the Quarter. He's a vampire and employs only vamps and one human to take daytime deliveries. He gives me info when he feels we need to know shit."

"Interesting," Paz replied. He pulled a comb out from his back pocket and combed his hair back. I noticed he was rocking a mullet and made a face.

"The Nineties called. They want their hairstyle back." I pointed at his head.

My fellow brothers laughed.

Face clapped me on the shoulder. "Sorry to burst your bubble, but that shitty-ass hairstyle is back in."

"Fuck," I murmured.

"Fucking awesome is more like it," Paz replied, replacing the comb back into his rear pocket with a cheesy grin, then he flipped Face and I both middle fingers.

Viper cleared his throat. "Terrible, all of you. Just awful." He swiped a hand down his face in annoyance. "Anyway, Theo's got a witch on his payroll and says she detected magic in the ashes they found outside his club last night."

"Vampires are, essentially, magic, though," Venom chimed in. "Same with wolves. So how did they know witches were involved in the vampire deaths?"

"A sorceress's signature," Viper replied. "That's what he said, anyway."

I made a mental note to ask Bloome about this magical signature next time I saw her. But when would that be? Fuck… why was I thinking about her at all?

"So… what? We're going to just hunt down this witch and kill her?" Phoenix asked, his massive arms folded across his cut.

"Absolutely not. She's to be brought in alive. For questioning." Viper cocked his head to the side and stared at the fire user.

I knew "questioning" meant "torture" if need be, and I was good with that.

"Darn," Phoenix replied, biting back a smile.

Violent asshole.

"Okay, where do we start looking?" I asked, wondering how we were going to track down this witch without a witch of our own on the payroll.

"We'll head to Zombies, see if Venom can get a scent," Viper said, heading for the door.

"Always the bloodhound," Venom grunted.

"Thanks for coming," Theo replied, shaking Viper's hand.

Theo was a little bit older, probably in his forties when he was turned, and was dressed in an expensive-looking suit and tie. Despite the loud and rowdy atmosphere of Zombies, Theo obviously took his job as owner of the club seriously. He must have a good head for business because the place was busy as hell for a Wednesday night. He had to be doing thousands a night in sales. The fact that Zombies was one street away from Bourbon Street surely didn't hurt.

"When did you discover the remains?" Viper asked as we began to walk toward the back of the club.

"My daytime guy, Gil, reported it to me when I got here at six. Said they were there when he opened up around noon, waiting on a few deliveries."

"And obviously they weren't there last night when y'all closed?" Phoenix asked.

"Not at all. It must have happened between four a.m. and noon. Not sure what vamps would be doing out past sunrise, which makes me wonder if they were led out into the sun."

Very strange indeed, I agreed in my head.

"But I didn't touch anything," Theo continued as he led us to the small alleyway behind the bar. "I was going to collect the remains before a big rain or wind came along but didn't when you said to leave it." He looked at Viper.

"You did good, thank you. We'll get rid of it."

"The clothes aren't singed so they didn't burn up in the sun," I pointed out.

"Took the words right out of my mouth," Phoenix replied.

Viper looked at Theo. "Did your witch say anything about who could have done this?" Viper asked.

Theo shook his head. "No, she just said it definitely was a witch who killed all three, and that she has a very specific 'sorceress's signature.'" He put up air quotes with his fingers.

"Interesting," Viper replied. He glanced at me and I could tell he was thinking the same thing I was: The witch *did* know who did it and isn't telling. No way she could tell a specific "signature" but not whose. All the witches knew each other around here.

"Okay, well thanks for your time. We'll do some investigating." Viper shook Theo's hand again.

Theo glanced at Venom, then to all of us, then wandered into the back door of Zombies.

Venom ignored him and bent down to grab a pinch of ash.

"He's lying or she's lying," I said quietly to Viper.

Viper nodded. "I think the witch is lying. Theo's always been on the up and up."

"It's definitely female and human or witch. Not vampire,"

Venom said, rubbing the ash between his fingers as he sniffed.

I made a face. "Those are the remains of a vampire, not an extinguished campfire. Have some respect."

Venom looked at me and his eyes flashed yellow for a quick second like they did when he was angry. "I'm being as respectful as I can. What else would you have me do? Get on my hands and knees and sniff it? Ya know what, don't answer that, dickhead."

"Can't you use the clothing?" I pointed to a man's shirt on one of the ash piles.

He shook his head. "No, the magic the witch used to kill the vampires is what would be in the remains, not really the clothing. Those will give me the vampires' scents, mostly."

I guessed that made sense.

"Stop busting his balls," Viper said next to my ear in a low tone.

I simply nodded.

Venom clap-swiped his hands back and forth to clear the ash. "It's faint but we can try. Follow me."

We really did treat him like a bloodhound. Oh well, he came in handy, and if we had to have a wolf in our MC, then I could think of way worse ones. Most of my club brothers knew how I felt about wolves—not that any of them were exactly fans of the mangy beasts either—but I was probably the worst of the haters.

"Collect this respectfully, in separate bags, along with the clothing. Ask Theo for a broom, since we already brought bags. Then take it back to the clubhouse," Venom said to Paz and Jewel, pointing at the piles.

"Yes, boss," they replied in unison.

Venom led us back through Zombies, where we received a lot of startled looks and stares, and out through the front door. He walked away from Bourbon Street and east toward the quieter streets. Viper, Phoenix, Face, and I followed him in silence, until he stopped short in front of a wiccan supply store. Being that it was two a.m., of course the shop was closed.

"The scent stops here," Venom said, looking at us and pointing at the door.

"It's a witch surplus store. Think she owns it?" Phoenix asked everyone and no one in particular.

Face typed the name and address of the shop into his phone. "I'll run a full background on the owners, see what we can come up with."

"Perfect," Viper said. "Once we get a name, we bring her in."

"You mean we kidnap her," I said with a laugh.

"Something like that." He chuckled.

After walking back to Zombies and retrieving our bikes, we reached the clubhouse fairly quickly and wandered inside. Phoenix and I went to check on the Cobalt Room, which closed in an hour and a half, and Face, Viper, and Venom went into Viper's office to do some investigating.

We sat at our favorite table and Ally came over. "Your usuals?"

"Yes, sweetheart. Thanks." I winked at her.

After she walked off, I went to say something to Phoenix but stopped when I saw him stiffen and his eyes dart around the bar.

"You all right, bud?" I asked.

"Witch," he replied with a sneer.

I looked in the direction he was staring. A group of women sat at a corner table talking and drinking. Phoenix hated witches more than I hated wolves and could sense them.

"Which one?" I asked.

"Not sure. One of them for sure, though."

"Here you go," Ally said, setting down our drinks.

"Thanks," we replied.

"Holler if you want another." She left back to the bar area and we didn't even appreciate her walking away as we usually did since we were fixated on the witch table.

I downed my bourbon in one gulp. Phoenix didn't touch his gin.

"Let's go say hi," I replied with a smirk.

He nodded in agreeance and followed me to the table. The women stopped talking and pretty much froze when we approached.

"Hello, ladies. I'm Shadow and this is Phoenix. We're the owners. Are you having a good time tonight?"

A blonde with her tits spilling out of her white top looked up at us. "Yes, we are. Thanks for asking."

"Shadow and Phoenix," a brunette with lots of curls repeated. "Are those your real names?" she asked around a snigger as she eyed our cuts.

"No," Phoenix, whose real name was Gabriel, replied, his jaw bunching in annoyance.

"What are you guys, like some big biker gang? I didn't know bikers owned this place. Seems pretty classy," the blonde stated.

"They're much more than bikers."

We looked to see a pale, black-haired girl sitting at the other side of the table. Her eyes flashed purple quickly at us before going back to normal. So quickly no human would have noticed.

"What does that mean?" the blonde asked.

"Witch," Phoenix muttered, staring at the woman.

The brunette with the curls scoffed. "That's not very nice. Nora's very sweet."

"I'm sure she is," Phoenix replied. "In fact, I'd love some alone time with… what did you say your name was?"

She hesitated before answering, "Nora. And no. I'm not interested."

I stared deep into her eyes. "Of course you are, honey. Come with us. We just want to talk."

84

"That shit doesn't work on me, dickhead," Nora replied, folding her arms over her black long-sleeved shirt. She wore a bunch of necklaces with strange symbols on them.

"What shit?" the blonde asked.

I made a tsking sound. "Explain later or just come chat with us. Your choice. We can help them forget."

"Forget?" the curly-haired brunette asked.

Nora huffed and got up. She followed us back to the office and we closed the door.

"If you try to bite me, just know I drink hemlock tea daily. So, unless you want blood like acid, you'll keep your damn fangs away from me." She folded her arms across her chest.

I rolled my eyes. "We didn't bring you back here to snack on you. Besides, hemlock is only poisonous to humans so I call bullshit." I lifted my chin as I awaited her response.

"Not all hemlock. Now, what do you want?"

Phoenix pulled out a chair and pointed at it. "Sit."

"I prefer to stand," she replied.

"We don't fucking care." I pushed her down into the chair, forcing her to sit.

She glared at us but kept up the defiant body posture.

"Three vamps were killed in the Quarter last night behind Zombies. What do you know about it?"

She grinned. "Oh, how unfortunate. But why would I know anything? They probably got taken out by wolves or other vamps."

I snorted. "No. A witch did it."

"How do you know?" she asked.

I looked at Phoenix. We both hesitated but then decided to tell the truth.

Phoenix replied, "The remains have a witch's signature on them. A 'sorceress's signature' as we were told."

She shrugged. "Fuckers probably attacked her. Self-defense, it sounds like."

"Negative. Vamps don't go around just attacking witches," I said.

"Right. Is that what your little biker friends get told by the vampire community? Because that is wrong." She snorted.

Just then, Viper walked in. "What's going on?"

"Viper, this is Nora. Local witch. She was having a drink with some friends and we decided to have a little chat."

"Is that so?" he asked, looking at her.

"Viper," she jeered. "Poisonous snake. How fitting."

Phoenix smacked his hand on the desk. "Look, one witch can't take out three vamps unless she somehow impairs them."

"Maybe she did." Nora feigned boredom by staring at her fingernails.

"How?" Viper asked.

She scoffed. "Right. Like I'd tell you. Snake."

"Listen, we find any more dead vamps and find out a witch is going around killing them, there'll be a war. One I promise you and your friends will not win." I opened the door. "Spread the word, sweetheart. We'll be watching you. All the covens." I narrowed my eyes in warning.

"Whatever," she said, getting up and leaving the office. She didn't even go back to her human girlfriends, she just walked right out of the bar, at a very fast clip.

14

WITCH PROBLEMS

Bloome

As I sat in a coven meeting, my mind should have been on the business at hand. The vampires were threatening war over a few dead bloodsuckers, but the only vampire I couldn't stop thinking about was the one I couldn't have. For the past week, I continually chastised myself for sleeping with Craig so soon.

Of course he didn't want to see me again. He got what he wanted. It was just the way he left... so abrupt. Like he wanted nothing to do with me after. I kept replaying the conversation over and over in my mind, trying to remember if I had said or done anything to drive him away so fast. I could only recall my stupid comment about calling him crazy for talking about mates and relationships, which I said in a teasing manner, but he obviously took it another way. Maybe he wanted a relationship, but he honestly seemed more like a terminal bachelor to me. That was why I'd slept with him. I thought it would be fun—plus it had been way too long. But in the end, we had just made it too awkward, and I hoped I hadn't made him hate me.

"What about you, Bloome?"

I looked up to see Iliana, our coven leader, asking me a question. All eyes in the room were on me.

Crap.

I cleared my throat. "I'm sorry, what was the question?"

She huffed, and stray strands of long gray hair that had escaped her bun moved out of her face. "I was asking for volunteers to go talk to the vampires."

"We already did that," I replied. "Remember? It got us nowhere. They think witches are killing vamps, Nora told us, so maybe just find the witch who's doing it. Problem solved."

A collective gasp could be heard around the room as they all stared at me, appalled.

"What?" I asked.

"I said they *told* us witches were killing vampires. We don't actually believe that, do we?" Iliana asked me.

I shrugged. "How the hell should I know?"

Iliana stared at me for a hard minute, then continued to drone on about how to protect ourselves from vampires by drinking hemlock tea and all the other shit I'd heard all my life.

Brantley leaned over and whispered, "You were fucking one of them the other night."

I looked at him horror. "Excuse me?" Oh, my God... had he heard us?

"Don't try to deny it, sister. We all heard it."

Shit.

"How do you know it was a vampire? Maybe I picked up a human at a bar."

"Doubtful. I know you had your eye on that tall drink of water we met with at the Cobalt Room. I saw how y'all were lookin' at each other. Don't try to deny it." Then he looked angry. "Wait. He's the one who pinned me to the wall. Ya know what? I don't like him."

"Stop it. We'll talk later. We're in a meeting!" I pointed to Iliana, who was still blathering on about who knew what.

"Whatever. It's almost over, then you're gonna give me all the deets," he drawled.

"What deets? Sounds like you heard all you needed to. And then some." I covered my eyes with my hand and looked down into my lap with a head shake.

"If there are no questions, meeting adjourned," Iliana said.

"Well, thank fuck," Brantley said under his breath.

I slapped his arm with a laugh. "Stop it."

He looped his arm through mine as we left the yoga studio, the one Iliana owned. Sure, she held a few classes a couple of times a week, but it was mostly a front for her witchy stuff and secret shop in the back.

Our house was only a four-block walk. Our other roommates had decided to take the car and go do something else, so Brantley and I walked slowly back home. The weather was still warm, but it was nighttime, and a slight, cool breeze blew, as fall had just been ushered in. All Hallow's Eve was approaching quickly.

"So, give me the details," he said.

I laughed. "Nothing to tell, like I said. We had a good time, and then he left."

"Just like that?" Brantley asked.

"Yep, just like that. Poof, disappeared into thin air. Gone."

He threw his head back and laughed, his Adam's apple bobbing. "I'm sure it must have seemed like that if he left so quick."

I chuckled. "Oh, no, it didn't just seem like that. The guy can literally disappear into thin air."

He stopped walking, causing me to stop. "Get out!"

I shrugged. "Not joking. It's freakin' weird, I tell you."

"Holy shit..." We kept walking and talking. "Have you asked him how he does it?"

"No, I keep meaning to. We just keep getting... busy."

He giggled. "I bet you do."

I slapped his thin arm. "Not like that. Like we've been talking or, ah, doing other stuff, and I don't get a chance to ask him."

"Even witches can't do that. Right?" he asked. Brantley was still new to the supernatural world.

We turned the corner to the tree-lined street that took us to our big home. "I suppose they can with the right spell. But this seems to come natural to Craig."

"Vampire Craig. Cute," he replied.

"Shadow is what he prefers. His road name or whatever those bikers call it," I corrected.

"I like Craig better," he replied.

I laughed. "Of course you do. Anyway, sometimes when vampires are turned, they get a special gift. We haven't figured out how it happens, but it does. I know one of the other vamps in their biker club can create and manipulate fire without burning himself. I'm not sure about the rest."

"Well, that's just an unfair advantage," Brantley pouted.

"You're not lying." I nodded in agreement.

"So are you gonna see him again, or what?"

I stepped over a branch lying in the middle of the sidewalk. "Not sure if he wants that. Besides, it's just lust, anyway. Vampires and witches aren't mates."

"Because you want kids someday, right?" he asked.

We reached the front of the house, and I was first to walk up the path and onto the porch. The old wood creaked under our footfalls. After opening the door with my key, I wandered inside.

"Well, do you?" Brantley asked, following me into the kitchen.

"I don't know. I think so but not right now, I'm only twenty-six. I have time."

Brantley clapped me on the shoulder and said, "You definitely do. I want kids someday, I think. Raise them up right, not like that nightmare upbringing I had." He shuddered.

I knew he was raised in foster care, but I hadn't asked about his past. He'd tell me in time, I supposed. So instead, I pulled him into a side hug. "You'd make a great dad."

"Thanks," he said, gently pulling away to go to the fridge. "What do you want for dinner? It's my night to cook."

"Shrimp etouffee," I replied with a smirk as I started loading coffee grounds into the filter.

He turned around and looked at me "You would."

Brantley had taught himself to cook, and not just mac and cheese and hot dogs. He was an absolute master. I was gonna get fat if he cooked every night.

"Yours is the best," I said, encouraging him. "Plus they'll be leftovers for tomorrow."

"Not with the way you eat, sis!" he said, biting back a smile while he unloaded food from the fridge and piled it onto the massive granite and wood island in our kitchen.

"Hey!" I replied, pouring water into the machine and then flipping the button. "If the food was gross, I wouldn't be eating so much of it!"

He snorted. "Nice excuse."

"What's going on in here?"

I had been staring at the coffee, willing it to brew, when I heard the voice. I looked up to see Nora, one of my roommates, standing at the kitchen doorway, her hip propped up against it.

"Dinner," Brantley answered, turning on the gas burner under the pot of water he'd just set there.

"I see that. I also heard you two talking. Was it about that guy you were fucking last week? We all heard that." She smirked at me.

"I think she's talking to you, Brant," I said teasingly.

"I wish," he murmured.

I looked at her. "What about him?"

"You gonna spill the beans or what?" she asked, lifting the lid and peeking into the steaming skillet.

Brantley slapped her hand. "Don't touch."

"Why do you want to know? He was just a fuck. You should try it sometime."

Out of my five roommates, Nora was my least favorite. She dressed like a gothic witch, rarely smiled, and had shaved off her eyebrows like Marilyn Manson. It made her look creepy, and she always had negative vibes coming off of her in waves.

"I don't need sex with a man to make me feel better about myself," she replied dryly, retrieving a coffee mug from the cupboard.

Did she think she was gonna get some of my coffee after talking to me like that? To my relief, she went to the Keurig and brewed some hot water.

"I don't need it either. I was just bored and horny." I shrugged as I lied. Well, about the bored part.

I watched as Nora removed a small vial of purple powder from the pocket of her black dress and dumped it into the hot water. She replaced the cork on the empty vial, put it back into her pocket, then plunked two teabags from a box into the water. She added lemon and honey and stirred it pretty quickly.

"What is that?" I asked, bringing the hot coffee to my lips. I pointed to her dress pocket.

"Hemlock."

"Why do you take that? Do you think a vampire is gonna bite you?" I teased.

"Yes," she deadpanned, staring at me with her dark-brown eyes while stirring the tea.

"Why do you think that?" I asked, curious.

She cleared her throat and lifted her chin. "It's happened before, and it won't fucking happen again."

Brantley turned around. "Ew, that's nasty. What happened?" I just now noticed he wore an apron with the *Hocus Pocus* characters' faces on it. I bit back a smile.

"Yeah, what happened?" I asked, blowing on my hot coffee.

Nora looked between the two of us. "I was careless, locking up the shop after dark, wasn't paying attention. He pounced. Thankfully, I had sleeping powder in my pocket and was able to dump the whole vial on him right as he bit into my neck. I got away, but that will never happen again." Her face was stormy—angry.

"I'm sorry, that had to be very frightening," I said sincerely.

She pulled the two teabags out and set them on a pre-prepared paper towel, along with the stir spoon. "It was, and it won't happen again."

"But the hemlock will only hurt the vamp once he bites, so it could happen again," I pointed out.

"They smell it on your blood, they won't bite. And if they're young and stupid and still bite, then they'll get very sick and could die," she stated matter-of-factly before sipping her tea and staring at me.

"I see," I replied. I knew hemlock root hurt vampires, I didn't think it killed them. In fact, I was sure it wouldn't. I remember reading in the library a couple of weeks ago. Destroy the brain or heart. It probably just burned the shit out of their mouth and insides—to which they would heal.

"Is that true?" Brantley asked as he dug rummaged through the spice shelves.

"It is," Nora responded. She pulled out another vial from her pocket and held it out to me. "You should be taking some yourself. Dump it in your coffee, it's tasteless."

For whatever reason, the first thought that came to my mind was... if I slept with Shadow again, he might think I smelled bad since Nora said they can scent it on our blood. And if he wanted to bite me during sex—which I'd heard was mind-blowing—then the hemlock would hurt him.

God, I was so pathetic. However, I did take the vial from her. "Thanks." I held it up and put it in my pocket.

"You should take it now. Takes a while to build up in your system."

"Coffee's almost gone," I replied truthfully. "I'll get some pop or something and take it later. Where can I get more?"

"The greenhouse has hemlock root growing. It's marked." She pointed out the window to the backyard. Then, she turned around and went to leave the kitchen but stopped as she reached the doorway. "Those filthy biker vamps pulled me into a meeting with them the other day. Said witches are killing vamps, just like Iliana was talking about. So the more protected you are, the better." She inclined her head at the vial in my hand. "I gotta go to work. Be home late." Then she walked out.

She managed a wiccan store down in the Quarter that stayed open late.

"Damn, she's intense. Sucks the life right outta the room," Brantley said, waving his hand flamboyantly before pulling the lid off the large pot and stirring its contents.

Yes, she was. But little did she know that Shadow wouldn't hurt me. I got the feeling he would rather get hurt himself than hurt me.

My cell rang from my pocket and I looked at the screen: Cobalt Repairs. The vampires' bike shop. Shit, what did they want?

15

SHORT-LIVED BLISS

Bay City, Michigan – 1955

Life was good. Saundra and I had been married about four years and were talking about starting a family. My own family, especially my pop, liked to rub it in that kicking me out at eighteen had been the best thing for me. I still disagreed, as I could have used a place to stay while I established my career and found love. But, I digress.

Working at the automotive parts factory in town had been good for me. It was still hard physical labor, but I could handle it just fine. It had great union benefits and kept me in shape. I had started to grow a beard, but Saundra hated it, so I would shave it off, then try to grow it again until she protested.

We had a good sex life, and I was glad I had waited until I found the right one before I had done that with anyone. We'd been each other's firsts, and Saundra's doctor said she was as healthy as a horse and had great pelvic structure to carry many babies. I looked forward to becoming a dad someday. For now, we were just saving up our money to buy a house of our own. The two-bedroom apartment was spacious enough, but I wanted to give her the green lawn and the white picket fence she'd dreamed about as a girl. I'd already given her the wedding of her dreams and it was my goal to make all her dreams come true. She'd made me so happy, it was the least I could do. For now, she stayed at home doing sewing and quilting jobs for extra cash that she either stocked away in a coffee can on top of our fridge, or occasionally she would splurge on a manicure or a new blouse. I told her she could buy those things whenever she wanted, but she insisted she liked having her own money to buy it with. It made her feel proud. Which in turn made me feel proud. I loved a woman with a mind of her own. My brothers' wives sometimes seemed like mindless robots who did whatever their husbands told them to. Not my Saundra. We'd only had a couple of spats, and it was always over her telling me she wanted to do her own thing and wouldn't be told what to do. Since then, we'd always made decisions together and it seemed that approach worked much better for us. I'd been raised watching my father tell my mother, not ask her, what we were going to do. Where we'd spend Christmas. What restaurant we were eating at on a Saturday night. What she could and could not wear in public and to church. Since I was raised that way, I never knew how wrong that was. But, my mother never protested so perhaps she liked it. I'd never find out.

I hadn't been back in the woods in many years. After my attack on the shores of the lake that fateful night four years ago, I avoided any place wolves might be. Especially since the police claimed they had never found said wolf. It honestly made me want to take my wife and move out of Bay City altogether, but then I thought—this wolf could be anywhere. Or perhaps it was dead. I couldn't live in fear—I refused to live in fear.

I had, however, visited the lake several times. It was where I'd proposed to Saundra and no bad memory was going to overshadow a good one. On our anniversary every year, we went for a nice steak dinner at the same restaurant we had that night, then we went on a walk down the shore. I always presented her with a new piece of jewelry. Tonight would be no different. Since she already had a pearl necklace, a jade bracelet, and ruby earrings, I decided a ruby ring to match her earrings would be perfect. She was born in July and that was her birthstone, after all. She'd gushed about it after I'd given her the earrings last year. The fact she had asked me if I knew ruby was her birthstone had been cute. Who did she think I was? I was no dummy. I'd asked the jeweler in town to show me the July birthstone pieces. Still, she'd made me smile so much that day.

Bellies full, we walked hand-in-hand down the shoreline. The ring was burning a hole in my pocket, just as the other one had four years ago this very night. And just like that night, the moon was full and illuminated our walk much better than the previous years' walks.

"The moon is breathtaking reflecting off the water," Saundra said, squeezing my hand and using her free one to point at the lake.

I pulled our linked hands up together and kissed her knuckles. "I agree, my love."

She smiled at me.

"But I have a confession. I think you're more beautiful than the moon on the water. Breathtaking, as you say. You stole my heart and continue to steal my breath."

She smiled shyly and reached her hand up to touch my face. "I love you, Craig Walsh."

"I love you, Saundra Walsh." I kissed her under the moonlight. After breaking the kiss, I looked down at her and said, "I know you're expecting jewelry since it's our anniversary, but sorry. It's not in the cards for us this year, sweetheart."

A disappointed look colored her features before she recovered with one of her sweet smiles. "It's okay, baby. I would rather have a house than jewelry any day. I only wear it on special occasions."

With a grin, I lifted her right hand to my lips and discreetly slid the ring onto her finger, then kissed her knuckles again.

She yanked her hand from me and stared at the silver and ruby piece. "Oh, my stars! This is gorgeous, Craig!" She stared up at me with wide eyes. "You're such a trickster!"

"Gotcha!" I made finger-guns and shot her with them.

Laughing, she shook her head. "I will never trust you again."

"Good, I want to keep you on your toes, Mrs. Walsh."

I leaned down and kissed her again. I would never grow tired of kissing her, even here in public. Not that there were many people around on this late summer Monday night. I had no shame in public displays of affection. As we continued to kiss, my dick paid attention and I decided I should probably get her home before I laid her down in the sand and really put on a show for any people who happened by.

"Let's go home," I murmured against her lips. "I need you."

Breathily, she agreed with a nod.

As I grabbed her hand to lead her back to the parking lot, something knocked me to the ground. The déjà vu of hot, rancid breath in my nose caused a panic to swell in me. Drooling jaws of sharp teeth inches from my face, and I could barely register the screams from my bride.

"Help us! Someone help us!" Saundra screamed.

I punched the wolf in the face—it was the same wolf from four years ago, I was sure. He yelped and leapt off me. I had a brand new Smith & Wesson in my car, and at that moment, that was my only goal: To get to my car and waste this sonofabitch once and for all.

As I got to my feet, I went to grab Saundra and run with her back to the car but realized her screams had stopped. I looked frantically around and saw the wolf dragging her by the hair down the beach, her lifeless body not fighting or screaming.

I ran as fast as I could toward them. Once I reached the wolf, I grabbed it by the scruff of its neck and pulled it off of my wife. It growled and barked at me but ran off into the night toward a copse of trees.

I barely noticed.

Falling to my knees in the sand, I picked up Saundra, whose hair was swishing in the waves flowing in and out of the lake, and held her tight. Her eyes were closed, and her lips were parted, but she made no sounds or movement. Blood from a large, gaping hole in her throat ran in rivulets over my white dress shirt's sleeves and absorbed in the cotton.

"Saundra!" I screamed, shaking her. "Please! I'm here, sweetheart. I'm here. Please wake up. We'll get you to a hospital!"

A few people had gathered now, staring at us in horror, some of them crying.

An older man ran over to us and stopped short, falling to his knees in the sand. "I'm a doctor. What happened to her?"

"A wolf, it bit her. Oh, Jesus, please. Please help her!" I whimpered. "Please help my wife."

The doctor put his fingers to the side of her throat that wasn't torn to shreds and then picked up her lifeless wrist, holding his fingers there several seconds. With a frown, he grabbed her body from me and laid her in the sand before putting his ear over her chest.

The most remorseful and sorrowful look I had ever seen passed over his kind features before he said in a small, sad voice, "I'm sorry, son. She's gone."

I let out a wail so loud, the people nearby probably thought I was an animal myself. I laid my head on Saundra's body and sobbed.

16

COMPROMISE

Shadow

Church was in full session, and if I could sweat, I'd be in full *sweat* session.

All eyes on me, I said, "What?"

"You're the only one here with connections to a witch," Face said with a grin.

That pissed me off. "Bull-fucking-shit. I'm sure someone here has connections. I sure as fuck don't."

"Yes, you do. *Fuck*, being the operative word," Kovah said with a grin behind his annoying-ass sunglasses.

I flipped him off. He grinned even wider in return.

Nobody else spoke. They just stared at me expectantly. When I couldn't take the silence any longer, I said, "So, lemme get this straight. You want me to call a witch, who I've fucked once and don't even speak to, and ask her for a motherfuckin' favor?"

"Yes," Viper replied. "Sounds about right."

I stared at his smug ass, his human mate standing beside him with her slim arm wrapped around his waist.

"You can do it, Shadow," MyAnna said, smiling genuinely at me with her big brown eyes. "I have faith in you!"

Dammit... I supposed I wasn't the only one weak to her charms. She was just a tiny human who still believed there was good in the world. I envied her.

"What happened to the lead on the wiccan shop? Who owns it?" I asked in deflection.

Face said, "A woman named Jeanne Coulter. She's human. Practicing wiccan, like her religion, but told us she doesn't believe in actual witches."

A few people laughed.

"It was a dead end," Viper chimed in.

"But Venom said the witch's scent stopped there," I argued.

"Probably a customer. I'm sure many witches use the shop for their supplies," Face came back.

"Why can't Theo get that witch who told him a witch was involved in the first place to find this sorceress?" I asked, trying to stall.

"Did you miss the part in the conversation where we determined her to be lying or unreliable? She's not going to pony up a name without a lot of torture so that's a very last resort. Not to mention, I'd like to not fuck off Theo's connections." Viper lifted his chin.

After scrubbing a hand down my face and over my beard, I looked at Paz. "Go get me the shop phone."

He nodded and said, "Happy to, but it's cordless. It won't work in here. Only in the clubhouse and shop."

Being that we were in the Cobalt Room, yards away, I knew he was right. "Lead the way," I told the prospect.

I realized I was grateful the phone didn't work in the bar. I had a slight more bit of privacy in the smelly bike repair shop.

"Find her number," I ordered Paz.

He scrolled through the phone's incoming calls and said, "This is the only one I don't recognize."

I looked at the date of the call and it matched the date when she'd called the shop to schedule the witch meeting. I could only assume it was her cell phone.

Truth be told, I had thought several times of coming down here over the past week and getting this number to call her. Bloome had been on my mind way more than I cared to admit, and now that I was actually calling her, I was nervous as shit. And sorta angry. I wanted to contact her on my own timeline. Not because the club was desperate for witch help and I was under duress to do so.

"Hello?"

I took a deep breath and told myself to man the fuck up. "Bloome?"

"Yeah. Who's this?"

"Shadow. Craig. Is there someplace we can meet A.S.A.P.?"

She paused before responding, "To talk to or to fuck? Since I know you don't eat. Food."

Fucking-A! This chick. I had to bite back a smile at her sass. "Well, while I'd love to make you scream my name out again, this time is just to talk. If you're down with that."

She gasped, and I grinned that I'd gotten the desired effect. Two could play shock factor games. "First off, I did *not* scream out your name, you arrogant asshole. Secondly, what the hell do we have to talk about?"

She *so* did scream out my name. Didn't she? Knowing she wasn't the type to argue, I continued, "Witch business."

"If you're looking for whoever killed those three vamps, you're barking up the wrong tree. I don't know and neither does my coven. We just had a meeting about this, as a matter of fact."

I glanced at Viper, Phoenix, and Face, who were now in the shop standing next to me. I knew they could hear the other side of the conversation. Viper nodded at me to continue.

"I get it, but we still need to talk," I said.

"About what?" she asked. Except this time, I detected no sass or attitude. It was my "in."

"About us. And some other witch stuff. Please, Bloome. Just meet with me." I hated the desperation in my voice, but answers sometimes required sacrifices in pride.

I could hear her breathing, despite her lack of words. I'd learned over my long life just to be quiet when I needed answers. Humans tended to hate long silences, and since witches were basically humans who knew how to manipulate magic, I had to trust the silent discomfort would work on her.

Finally, she replied, but was sure she had food in her mouth as she mumbled around it, "Fine, where?"

"Cobalt Room. Right now, sweetheart." I hung up.

"Wow, harsh," Face said, laughing.

I glared at him, then looked at Venom. "She was eating. I have no patience for that shit."

"Wow, harsh," Venom mimicked Face a split-second before he shoved what I thought was an orange and black cupcake into his mouth.

I made a face. "Halloween cupcakes? Ew."

He swiped his hand over his beard and licked his lips. "Fucking delicious. Why would you fuckers ever choose blood over actual food? Sugar... nectar of the gods."

I pointed at his six-pack stomach hiding under his tee. "I don't know how the fuck you eat that shit and keep that physique."

"It's a wolf thing. You wouldn't understand," he said, grinning while licking white icing from his fingers.

I shook my head. "Nor would I want to. We didn't eat that garbage in the nineteen fifties when I was turned."

"Fuck, you're old!" Venom quipped, unwrapping another treat he'd somehow pulled out of nowhere. He bit into a pink and white pastry that made me want to gag at the sight.

I could barely remember eating human food... and what was it? Burgers, fries, and shakes at the local soda shoppe. Pork chops and applesauce at home growing up. Fried chicken and baked potatoes at the summer picnics and rodeos. A homemade apple pie or peach pie for a treat. None of that pre-packaged crap Venom was currently shoving into his maw.

And why was he called Venom, anyway? I still hadn't gotten the answer to that and made a mental note to ask him one day.

Without a look back, I snapped my fingers and found myself in the Cobalt Room at my favorite table. The ability to move from one place to another without walking was a weird fucking ability, but I'd grown used to it. Not by my own choice, but I'd embraced it just the same.

Her milky, freckled skin and defiant gaze had my dick twitching behind my pants. Fuck... I loved a woman with an attitude.

"Well, what do you want?" she asked.

"I hope we didn't interrupt your dinner," I replied, thinking about how she had been eating when I'd called.

She brought the wine glass to her lips that Ally had just delivered to our table inside the Cobalt Room. "Actually, you did. I was enjoying a nice shrimp etouffee when you called."

"From Mulate's?" I asked, somehow knowing that particular restaurant made the best etouffee.

"No," Bloome deadpanned. "My roommate is a hell of a cook. Better than any restaurant around."

"I find that hard to believe," MyAnna chimed in. I didn't even realize she was here until she spoke.

Bloome narrowed her eyes at the petite brunette. "Like I would take culinary advice from a vampire anyway."

"I'm human," MyAnna replied defensively. "And I used to work there."

I watched as Bloome licked her teeth behind closed lips and

flicked her gaze between Viper and his mate. She lifted her chin and narrowed her eyes at MyAnna. "For now."

Before Viper snapped, I sighed audibly and said, "Bloome, *please*. We need your help. To find a witch. How much power do you have?"

She grinned before setting her wine glass down. "How much money do you have?"

"So money equates to power?" I asked rhetorically, folding my arms across my cut. "I already knew that, sweetheart. I'm asking you a genuine question. We have cash and you have power so how much do we get for, say, ten grand?"

Her blue eyes went wide for a split second before she recovered. "Depends. What do you need to know?"

"Stop with the fucking games," Viper chimed in, scrubbing an exasperated hand down his face. "You gonna help us find this vampire-murdering witch or not?"

Bloome didn't break eye contact with my best friend. Which I'd give her credit for. Viper could be an intimidating sonofabitch when he needed to be. "Yes, I'll help, but I have conditions."

"What are they?" I quickly asked.

Bloome moved her gaze back to mine. "Complete anonymity. Nobody—and I mean nobody—knows that I helped you guys. The coven'll have my head if they find out I sided with the vamps. But I need the cash and I also believe in justice. So don't ask me any more fucking questions about my intentions and I'm down to help you find this witch."

I was good with that and hoped my club brothers were as well. I stared at them collectively and they all gave me slight nods of agreement.

"Well, now that that's settled, let's get down to it," I said, staring at the redhead who had already stolen my heart, even though I knew I could never have her. After all, love for a lifetime clearly wasn't in the cards for me and never would be. And I'd accepted that, as much as I didn't want to.

17

INTERROGATION

Bloome

L et's just keep it real… I was here because Shadow had asked me to be. Nothing more. If any of the other vampires had asked me to come to their creepy clubhouse and help them find the witch who'd been murdering their kind, I would have gladly held up both middle fingers and told them to sit-and-fucking-spin.

But Craig—Shadow—he had a hold on me. I wasn't sure he knew he did, but he did. My attraction to him was ridiculous and had clearly turned me into a pile of compliant goo, and for that, I was pissed. Turned on, aroused, and floaty in my brain, but still pissed.

Who did he think he was? Manipulating me like that?

Who did I think I was, letting him do so?

Truth was… I had power, real witch power, but as I'd told Craig a few weeks ago, I was still a lesser witch. At only twenty-six years old, I was considered a baby in the witch world. After all, our powers didn't come to us until we turned eighteen. Powers I knew would be arriving and powers I'd studied for. My mother's a very powerful greater witch, and in about four years, I would be like her. My father's a warlock, and I had acquired his powers, as well. Lots of witches tended to mate with humans, which lessened and muted the strength of their offspring, but no… not my mom. She'd found the most powerful warlock around and had made him her baby daddy.

But here I was… a formidable witch, still coming into my powers, and falling for a vampire, one I knew couldn't give me children. I made a mental note to call up Mom and ask her what the hell that was about. I knew I'd get an ass-chewing, but I didn't care. I needed to know why I was so cosmically drawn to this otherworldly creature who everyone knew couldn't procreate.

Babies… a relationship with a vampire… where had my head gone? Why was I even thinking about this? I was here, at this vamp den, to do a job. One that would put ten grand into my pocket. Add to the stash of cash I already had and help me buy a little house on the outskirts of New Orleans so I could be alone and not deal with covens, roommates, and most of all, fucking vampires.

"So… tell us, Bloome. This sorceress's signature… whose is it?" the one called Viper asked me.

I had prepared for this. I knew they were looking for the witch who'd killed those three behind Zombies, and I already had a sneaking feeling I wouldn't have too hard of a time tracking her down, but I needed something to go on.

"I'm gonna need something personal," I replied, talking to Viper but staring at Shadow, who stood amongst a bunch of other vamps.

Goddamn, were these guys huge. Next to him stood a redhead who was almost as tall as Shadow, tattoos covering his massive biceps while fire danced on his palm—fire he seemed to almost be playing with. Next to him was the prettiest man I'd ever seen, sculpted arms, flat stomach, perfect hair, lips, jawline… flawless skin and beautiful eyes and eyelashes that were looking down at his electronic tablet. As my gaze moved away from the modelesque vamp, an equally as tall guy with black hair, dark sunglasses, and some very unusual tattoos stood there munching on a banana. Which I found extremely odd since I knew vampires didn't eat.

I didn't have the energy to question this, so I moved my gaze back to Shadow, who was still staring at me with amusement, and dare I say lust in his silvery-gray gaze.

"Now that you've gotten your fill of my club brothers, are you ready to get to work, Bloome baby?" Craig asked me.

Pissed off and embarrassed he'd caught me checking out the other vamps, I narrowed my eyes at him. "Of course."

"Perfect. Now, how much juice do you have to track down a witch's—a sorceress's—signature?"

This was definitely a trick question. I'd been thinking long and hard about the dead vamps behind Zombies I'd heard about, and that a witch had been responsible, but I hadn't been able to get a lead on who'd done it. That being said, I knew my very powerful witch mother or my warlock father could help me. I just wasn't ready to call on them just yet. I'd always prided myself on being stubborn and self-sufficient, even if I was still a lesser witch.

So, I decided on something in between. "I have a lot of juice, and I can definitely tell you which witch it was… ha." I smiled at my own witchy pun. The vampires did not find this amusing at all. I cleared my throat and continued, "However, there is a protection spell I have to perform first in order to not be caught out by my coven. They tend to get a little… ah… testy when they think a fellow witch is going against their rules."

"Rules…" Shadow stared at me questioningly.

"Yes, rules, Craig. I'm sure y'all have rules as well," I snapped, looking around at the vamps circling me.

The whole situation was intimidating, and truth be told, I really didn't want to be here. I wanted to help Craig, but I didn't want to be a traitor to my coven, and everything inside of me screamed that I should not be helping any fucking vampires. That my feelings for Shadow were over*shadow*ing my judgement. Ugh.

"Tell me about your rules," Viper asked, staring at me with those light hazel eyes. I glanced behind him to see his tiny mate gripping onto him. She claimed she was human. Was she just going to grow old and die while he watched?

Who effing cares?

"We're to remain true to our coven. The witches and warlocks.

Not help vamps. But being that you think witches are killing vampires, I'm willing to get to the bottom of it and hopefully prove it wasn't a witch."

"And if it was a witch?" Viper asked.

"I'll be truthful either way," I replied honestly. Little did they know that if it was a witch doing this, the coven would handle doling out the punishment, not these neanderthals.

"What do you know of magical signatures?" Shadow asked me as he stared deep into my eyes. I had to resist squirming under his intense gaze, as all I wanted to do was leave here and have him take me to his room, and wrap me in his arms, and make me feel protected. Since when had I wanted a vampire to make me feel protected, I didn't know, but the strange emotion wouldn't leave my brain—and heart.

Gathering my composure, I said, "A little bit. Bring me something personal and I'll try."

A young-looking guy with a mullet responded to Viper's command to "go get the bags" and disappeared into a door set off on the side of the warehouse. They had me in a chair set in the middle of their warehouse they referred to as a clubhouse. The tall, intimidating men—vampires—stood around me and said nothing.

The one who'd been munching on the banana approached me. "How long have you been a witch?"

"My whole life," I quickly replied. "Why do you care?"

"Do you have any plans on becoming a vampire?" he asked, pulling out chew from his pocket and popping a wad into his mouth.

I wrinkled my nose. I glanced at Craig then back to his sunglassed friend. "Absolutely not."

"Good. Because I kill anything that turns into a succubus." The guy saluted me before walking away.

I rolled my eyes. "Good to know, douchebag."

My eyes cut to Shadow and his fire-using friend as they snorted a laugh.

The mullet vampire plonked a bag onto my lap. I looked down to see it contained a good amount of ash and some clothing. I looked up at Viper. "You want me to do what with this?"

"You asked for personal effects, sweetheart," Shadow quickly responded.

"Yeah, of the witch, not of dead vamps," I snapped, pointing at the bag on my lap.

Shadow looked at me, incredulous. "What on earth made you think we had any personal effects of the witch?"

"You said a witch did this. If she didn't leave evidence behind, how do you know it was, in fact, one who killed them?" I pointed to the bag again.

"Another witch told us," Viper said vaguely.

I huffed. "Then why not just get her to get you this information?"

"You ask too many questions," Viper came back.

"A witch killed them, and her signature is in the ash, so we were told," the fire-user replied, staring at me with freaky yellowish-green eyes. I looked down at this name patch and saw "Phoenix."

"Okayyy," I replied, gingerly opening up the bag and looking inside. I lifted my hand to activate magic and nothing happened. I tried again, but no colorful sparks would appear.

"Uh, slight problem. Your club is warded against witches using magic, isn't it?"

"Fuck," Shadow said. "That's right." He looked at Viper. "Can we turn it off somehow?"

Viper shook his head. "No, let's go outside."

I struggled to lift the heavy-ass bag and Shadow easily lifted it from me. I followed the huge vampires through the bike shop. Once inside, I immediately felt magic coming from the bag. "Stop!" I said.

They all stopped walking and looked at me.

I told Shadow to set the bag on a repair table and opened it back up. I could definitely feel some sort of magical presence, and it wasn't vampiric. The clothes were intact, which told me they weren't burned alive, but the ashes were the result of a witch's power.

I activated my magic, and colorful sparks began dancing on my fingertips. Putting my face over the bag, I closed my eyes and gave it a big whiff. Witch pheromones, combined with a strong scent of hemlock assaulted my nose.

Crap.

I slowly opened my eyes and looked at the intimidating vampires surrounding me. "There's definitely a sorceress's signature on these remains, and I'm fairly sure I know the witch who did this."

They stared at me expectantly as I hesitated to deliver Nora a death sentence.

"Well, give us a name, sweetheart," Craig said.

My stomach did a flip-flop as I looked into his beautiful face. I wanted to run my fingers over his beard before sitting on that face and screaming out his name. Instead, I cleared my throat and said, "I'll tell you when I have hard proof, and then after that, I need to bring it to the coven first."

"No," Shadow said, looking angry. "Tell us who you think did this."

"Sorry, Craig. That's not how we operate. Once I'm one hundred percent sure it's who I think it is, the coven will dole out the punishment—not you guys."

"I thought you said your coven would frown upon you working with vampires," Craig commented.

"Yeah, they're gonna hand me my ass, but now that I think I know who did this, and that we know her, this changes the game."

"Punishment… like what?" Phoenix asked.

"That'll be discussed at a later date," I replied, leaning against the table and folding my arms across my chest after shaking my hand to clear the magical sparks.

Shadow and I stared hard at each other for a few long seconds. Then he said, "You're not getting a dime until we get a crack at this witch after you hand down your 'punishment.'"

"What, like kill her? I definitely will not agree to that." I narrowed my eyes at him.

"She killed three of our own, plus who knows how many more. She's as dangerous as an animal and should be put down like one," Viper replied, his face stormy, a large V appearing between his eyes.

While it didn't surprise me that they wanted her dead, I wasn't sure I could live with myself if I handed her over to be executed. I left the bag on the table and walked toward the shop's door. "If she confesses to Iliana and the coven council, then we'll hear her side of the story. If she killed in self-defense, I'm sorry to inform you that she'll be dealt with but there will be no torture or harsh punishment, and certainly no killing."

I went to walk out of the shop and looked at Shadow and the guy with the sunglasses. "That goes double for you two!" I pointed at them.

18

TRAGIC VENGEANCE

Bay City, Michigan – 1955

My clammy hands were doing me no favors. The harder I gripped the gun, the worse my palms started to sweat. It was my third month out here and I had yet to find that fucking wolf who had stolen my entire world from me.

I'd gone completely mad after Saundra's death. They'd locked me in a mental hospital for a month—straightjacket and everything—but I didn't care. It gave me lots of time to think about how I was going to kill that goddamn wolf and in which manner I was going to do it.

Once I proved that it was just grief that had caused me to go a little nutty, they let me out. The factory had fired me—which was disappointing and hurtful. They had always said their employees were family, but I supposed that was just a line to keep us working there. They hadn't cared about me at all, delivering my pink slip to my home mailbox without so much as a, "I'm sorry for your loss."

My parents were sympathetic to my plight but had no idea how to handle me. I barely spoke to my family. I spent most of my time in the library researching werewolves. As I had sat in that sterile, padded room, all the radio shows and comic books I'd listened to and read as a teen came back to me. "The Wolfman" was the one that stuck out the most. Except this wolf wasn't half-man, half-beast. No, the fucker that killed my bride was just a plain wolf. But it definitely understood English and knew to run when the police were coming or when the doctor and the other passersby had approached. It hadn't attacked them. It hadn't attacked anyone else except me and Saundra. Almost like it was personal.

After poring over encyclopedias and old books on legends and lore, I knew exactly what I was going to do when I found this bastard.

First of all, werewolves only came out during the full moon, and that was why I found myself sitting in the sand on the shore where it had attacked us four months ago. One month in the asylum, and after that, I'd come out here every full moon for the past three months, waiting for it to show its ugly mug. I'd begrudgingly had to melt down some of Saundra's jewelry for the pure silver, but was rewarded with eight silver-dipped bullets, which were now loaded into my Smith & Wesson. I definitely wasn't going to kill this wolf quickly. No, I was going to make it suffer while I delivered a preplanned monologue about how its actions had ruined my life.

The past three full moons had yielded nothing. I sat out here each night, three nights a month during the full moon, but it hadn't showed. Tonight, I tried a different approach. I'd parked my car, which thankfully was paid for since I was now homeless—evicted from my apartment since I'd had to use my savings to pay hospital bills and burial costs for my wife—as close as I could to the water and waited. During my last visit to my parents' house, I'd swiped my dad's bird-watching binoculars without his knowledge and used them now to see if this wolf would show up again. It was the last night of the full moon and if it didn't show up tonight, I'd have to spend another month coming up with a better plan.

Scanning the trees, shoreline, and parking lot, I saw nothing. I sat there for hours, waiting, and nothing. As dawn began to approach, I started up the car, frustrated but determined to find this murderous beast eventually.

I steered the car toward the woods, where I'd slept those few nights after getting booted out of my parents' house six years ago and parked the car. I again found myself living in the woods, but this time, I had better equipment, a tent and sleeping bag that kept me warm and lots of matches for campfires, a bow and arrow to hunt for food, and my dad's fishing pole he'd "loaned" me that he probably wouldn't be getting back.

Scrubbing a hand over my quickly growing beard and too-long hair, I trekked toward my campsite, my revolver tucked snug in my trouser pocket.

After starting a fire, I let it smolder while I went to a nearby stream to catch fish for dinner. It didn't take me long to score two trout. I'd taught myself to gut and cook fish, and once it was cooked well enough, I pulled the pieces apart and scarfed down my dinner. What I wouldn't do for some broccoli and a baked potato right about now.

I knew I needed to go find a job—anything—to support myself, but I just couldn't think that far ahead. I needed to find this wolf and end him. I couldn't get closure until it was dead, and I had to be the one to do it.

After cleaning up dinner, I plucked the novel I'd swiped from the library out of my backpack and set it on my sleeping bag, intent on reading before bed, the big, full moon my nightlight. The forest was quiet, crickets chirping and the occasional branch crack as small forest animals scurried around.

Fall was approaching quickly, and I wondered how I'd do out here during a Michigan winter, but I told myself I'd cross that bridge when I came to it. After doing a crude tooth brushing with some toothpaste I still had on hand, and a bird bath in the stream, I went to my tent and unzipped my sleeping bag. A crack of a branch caught my attention, but I didn't think too much of it.

The feral growl, however, wasn't something I could ignore.

I immediately snatched my revolver from under my pillow and exited the tent. As if my prayers had been answered, there stood the gray wolf, ten feet away, staring at me, snarling.

My blood instantly boiled. It was the same wolf—I was sure of it. With my thumb, I cocked the hammer back on the gun and pulled the trigger, firing it straight into the beast's flank. It didn't even have a chance to run. It fell to the forest floor with a yelp and squirmed in place.

I ran over to it, smoking gun in my hand, and cocked the hammer back again as I hovered over it. Then, something I would never, ever forget happened. It was like it happened in slow motion. The wolf's fur began to retract into its body, its long snout shrinking into its face. Where there was once long black claws were fleshy hands. And within seconds, where a wolf once lie was a naked human man with a bleeding gunshot to the area between his hip and thigh.

"Holy Jesus!" I breathed, taking a step back but keeping my very shaky hand holding the weapon trained on the man.

"Help me," he whimpered, rolling over and sliding a hand over the wound.

I didn't know what to do. I'd read about this in all those books, but a part of me didn't actually believe this was true. How was this possible? A human being turning into a wolf, or vice-versa?

"Don't help him."

I whipped my head around to see three males emerge from the forest. They were extremely pale under the full moon. At this point, I wasn't sure where to aim the gun.

"What? Who are you?" I asked the strangers, who all wore dark-colored coats, jeans, and sported James Dean type hairstyles.

"Help me," the wolf-slash-man at my feet said.

Anger took over my confusion, and I kicked the man in the stomach. "Start talking, you louse! Why did you kill my Saundra?"

One of the pale men laughed. "That's not gonna work on a werewolf, man."

I narrowed my eyes at the trio. "Who are you? Where did you come from?"

"Saundra... you took her from me," the wolfman said, rolling back over to his side.

One minute, the trio of pale men were ten feet away, the next they were standing two feet from me. I jumped back. "What the heck!" I pointed the revolver at them.

There was too much going on, and I was so confused. "I don't know who you are but please leave. This is between me and this man right here."

"He kill someone you love?" the tallest of them asked me.

I nodded. "My wife. Tore her throat right out in front of me." I bit back a sob, as I didn't want to appear weak in front of these men, whoever they were.

"Then shoot him again, make him suffer. Or, I can start breaking his limbs for you. Or his neck…"

I looked at the pale man. "No, I've got this under control. I don't know where you came from, but just go."

"Saundra…" the man whimpered.

I bent down and pressed the barrel of the gun to his temple. "Say my wife's name one more time, and I'll waste you."

"You took her from me," he said.

"Who are you?" I asked, my teeth grinding together.

"She was to be mine, not yours, you thief," he said quietly.

"Just waste him already. Filthy wolf has no use on this planet," one of the pale men said.

I turned the gun on him. "I said, shut up!" I felt like I was about to crack and kill everyone around. There was too much going on in such a short period of time and my brain couldn't keep up.

"Saundra was nineteen when I met her. She hadn't loved anyone before me. And then you killed her." I pressed the muzzle harder into his temple, the tears I couldn't hold back now falling like rain down my cheeks. "I hate you. I hate you so much!"

"His wound is going to heal if you don't off him. Let me take his head off. Those bullets won't kill him either."

I looked over at the pale man and said, "Shut your trap. *Please* just shut your trap." I shook uncontrollably now, sweat and tears mixing on my face.

I looked back at the naked man. "These are silver bullets. You want another?"

"No, please," he whimpered.

"Smart, very smart," the pale man said, smiling, and I just now noticed he had fangs that shone under the full moon.

Fangs… what the?

"Get the fuck out of here!" I screamed, knowing I'd finally lost the plot since I'd used the F-word.

"He won't heal, I stand corrected," one of the pale men replied.

I lifted the gun and shot him in the stomach. He fell to the forest floor, gripping his stomach with a curse.

Hot, stinging heat seared into my leg. I looked down to see the man was a wolf again, and his fangs were clamped onto my calf.

"Get off me!" I screamed.

Then he lunged up and snapped his mouth on my neck. Remembering I had the gun, I cocked the hammer back and shot the wolf in the head. Blood and bone splattered my face. He immediately dropped to the forest floor, changed back into a man, and lay lifeless and unmoving. He died with his eyes open.

Two of the pale men advanced on me so fast, I didn't see them coming.

The weapon slipped from my hand as both men bit into the side of my neck and chewed my skin, muscles, and veins to shreds. I could literally feel my lifeforce draining out of me… and pretty much couldn't care less.

At least I'd die happy, knowing I'd murdered the sonofabitch who'd taken my Saundra from me.

19

BSI – AGAIN?

Shadow

"What a gem she turned out to be," Kovah snarked, spitting chew into a Styrofoam cup.

I narrowed my eyes at him. "Are you still fucking here?"

"I was just leaving," he replied with a chuckle before letting himself out through the front door to the clubhouse. The overhead alarm chirped twice, letting us know the door had been opened.

Phoenix clapped me on the shoulder. "Don't listen to that immature asshole. I think Bloome will come through for us. I saw the way she looked at you. She's definitely got it bad for you."

I laughed sardonically and said, "Thanks, brother. But I doubt it. I'm fairly sure she hates my guts. But everyone's got a price. She'll hand over the murderous witch to us if she wants her ten grand."

Phoenix grinned, his yellowish-green eyes dancing with mischief. "I can't argue with you there."

"So, you both agree that the redhead will be of no use to us," Venom remarked as he walked into the kitchen where Phoenix and I sat, discussing the meeting with Bloome. He opened the refrigerator door and rummaged around before pulling out a loaf of bread, two bottles of condiments, cheese, and lunchmeat.

God, it must be such a burden to have to constantly feed the human body. After sixty-plus years, I could hardly remember what that was like. A sustenance of blood was much easier to maintain.

"I wouldn't say no use…" I started to defend her but realized I couldn't. Not really. Bloome hadn't promised us shit, and for that, I was annoyed and honestly, a bit embarrassed. "But yes, hopefully she'll give up a name and we can get rid of this murderous witch. We need to maintain peace in the city."

Venom finished assembling his sandwich and then plucked an orange from the basket on the counter and began peeling it. "You do realize those witches have been in this area for decades… centuries. You vamps coming here and telling them how things are gonna be isn't going over well with them."

"We get what you're coming from, dawg, we really do, but you don't think Viper did his homework? There was already an established community of supes when we got here. The vampires mostly laid low, with not a lot of leadership. They were happy to let the Nighthawks take the reins. That's no bullshit," Phoenix said.

Venom tossed the orange peels in the trash and plucked a wedge from the fruit. He popped it in his mouth before answering. "I have no doubt Viper did his homework, but you still need to understand that vampires aside, the rest of the supes were living and thriving here just fine before we rolled into town. Witches, wolves, hell even the faeries and dragons were doing fine—and they still are."

I shook my head and raked my fingers over my too-long beard. "Faeries and dragons… you know what? I don't even wanna know. We'll talk about that later. All I can tell you, from what my best friend has told me, is that the vamp community here in the Big Easy was an unorganized mess. And we're here to clean it up. Or at least give it a small facelift."

Venom stared at me as he continued to shove orange slices into his mouth but said nothing.

"As far as I'm concerned, we can clean it up, get some organization going, and keep the peace, not only in the Quarter, but most of the South. We've got the Shreveport club still going strong, and we can branch out to other areas once we're ready." Phoenix folded his arms across his chest and stared at the werewolf.

Venom piled his sandwich together and smashed it flat with his huge, meaty hand on the cutting board. Then, he lifted it to his lips and paused before saying, "I definitely can't fault you for having a plan."

As he bit into it and chewed, I continued, "Hey... I've been meaning to ask you, how did you get the name Venom, anyway?"

He swallowed down the bite of his sandwich and said, "It's a long story."

"Okay?" I said. "Does it have anything to do with being a wolf?"

Venom smacked his hands together to clear the crumbs, then raked a hand through his salt-and-pepper beard to clear the rest. "I'll tell you the story one day."

I shrugged. "I have nothing but time."

I must have looked sad about that because he replied, "I've accepted my monthly curse. Have you accepted your eternal one?"

I nodded. "Sixty years and counting, brother. No thanks to one of your kind."

Venom pierced me with an intense stare before nodding in respect and exiting the breakroom eating his sandwich.

I let out a breath I didn't know I was holding and looked at Phoenix, who was staring at me with raised eyebrows. "What?" I asked.

"Ya gotta cut him some slack, man," he said.

"Oh, okay. I will once you accept that we need to work together with the witches."

I wasn't one hundred percent sure on his past with witches, but I knew it was sour and jaded, so I used his hatred toward them against him every chance I could.

He folded his massive arms across his chest, and with his eyes narrowed, he replied, "I'll tolerate them but never accept them as allies."

I bit back a smile. "Really? Even if they prove themselves?"

His pale cheeks flushed, and it had been a long time since I'd seen a vampire's face get that red. "Witches can never be allies. I only joined this club for a place to belong, but if y'all are going to be aligning yourselves with the likes of witches, then I'm fucking out."

I'd never heard Phoenix talk like that, nor be so passionate about something. I reined in my snark and tried my hardest to soften my features. After all, it had taken everything in my gut to accept Venom into our club, but I liked to believe I had evolved over the past sixty years to realize they weren't all bad. I hoped one day Phoenix would realize that about witches. One of them had wormed her way into my heart and I wasn't sure what I would do if I decided to make her my mate and had to humbly ask that my club brothers accept her.

I ran my fingers over my long, dark beard and stared at my friend, who had hurt dancing in his jaded gaze. "I don't think the Nighthawks will ever fully align with witches, but in this day and age, we need to learn to try to coexist. Don't you think so?"

Phoenix stared at me long and hard before nodding. "I do."

I grinned. "See? Was that hard?"

He bit back a smile. "Thanks for talking me off the ledge. Probably won't be the last time."

I chuckled and pulled him into a man hug. I knew the fucker was over a hundred years old and that constantly having to evolve and adapt could wear someone down. After pulling back, I said, "You weren't on a ledge. I can tell you've been fucked over by a witch—probably a sorceress—and you're angry. One day I hope to get your story. Until then, you have a family here with the Nighthawks. Just like you pledged all those years ago. Vampires first… it will always be our motto. Nighthawks protect their own. Nothing comes between us and the world. Nothing." We bumped fists in agreement.

"Visitor!" Dash's voice.

Phoenix and I turned our heads toward the noise to look at the video mount in the corner of the breakroom. It seemed the Bureau of Supernatural Investigation—the damn BSI—was once again visiting the Cobalt Room.

What the hell did those cops␣what want?

"Fuck. Let's get over there. See if Viper needs backup."

Phoenix agreed as we headed toward the walkway that led us to the Cobalt Room.

I should have found it odd that Kovah and Special Agent Bishop were huddled together in the corner of the bar, but I didn't. Viper had told me they had history dating back years. Everyone knew Kovah was a vampire-human hybrid who didn't age, could resist the sun, and eat human food, but we knew little of his actual past. Looking at Special Agent Bishop, and knowing he was human, I could tell he couldn't be older than thirty and determined that Kovah's history with the agent had to be recent.

Not that I fucking cared at the moment.

"What do they want?" I asked Viper, who had his woman pressed up close to his front.

"I don't know but get rid of them. I have an announcement to make, and their appearance here is cock-blocking it."

Both eyebrows hit my hairline. I'd rarely heard my friend talk like that and it was fucking awesome. I swaggered over toward Kovah and Special Agent Bishop. They stopped talking when I approached.

"What do you want, Special Agent?" I asked the blond agent.

"Just a routine check of the bar. Everything looks great. No worries." He tried to throw me a charming Southern grin, but I saw right through it.

I sucked in my cheeks and then blew out a breath. "Okay, cool. So you'll be leaving now?"

"Once I'm done chatting with my friend." He pointed at Kovah. "Yes, I will."

Seemed harmless enough, and I walked away. I was too old for their immature shit, so leaving the scene was the easiest thing anyway.

"How long do you plan on waiting to call Bloome before you cave for some answers?" Phoenix asked me.

I glanced at him to see a knowing smile dance on his lips. Smarmy bastard.

"Two days. She doesn't get with us about this murderous witch, I bust down her door and find her myself. It's not like I don't know where she lives."

We watched as Kovah walked Special Agent Bishop to the door and then locked it, as the bar was now closed.

"Everyone have a seat," Viper said, standing against the bar with his woman.

I knew he had something to say tonight, so I took a seat at our favorite table next to Kovah. Phoenix and Venom did as well.

"MyAnna and I are engaged to be married. We're going to do it right here, along with her turning ceremony so we can be together forever. I expect all of you to be there as I make her my old lady."

She shoved at him playfully while holding out a ridiculously large diamond ring on her left hand. The place erupted in claps and we made our way to the front of the bar.

Jewel was the first to approach. She grabbed MyAnna's hand and examined the ring, whistling low under her breath. "Wow, that's a beaut. Perfect clarity. Pure."

"Hands off. In fact, eyes off," Viper said, eyebrow raised.

Jewel raised both hands in surrender and laughed. "I would never."

I couldn't stop the smile on my face. I had never seen Vane this happy. I smacked him on the back with a hug and congratulated them both. "I never thought I'd see the day," I said to my best friend.

"Me either," Viper said, unable to hold back a smile. One I hadn't seen in many years. "You'll be my best man, right?"

"I better be!" I replied.

20

MORAL DILEMMA

Bloome

I paced back and forth on the rug beside my bed. Finger to my mouth, I racked my brain for a decision that wouldn't leave Nora dead or me with a guilty conscience. As far as I could see, I had two choices: Approach Nora and ask her straight up if she killed the vampires behind Zombies and any others. Or I could go to Iliana with the evidence and let her sort it out. The last thing I was going to do was just hand her over to a den of undead vipers, as much as she annoyed me most of the time.

I just had to wonder what her motive was. Had she truly been defending herself? I was sure, when asked, that would be her response. It would definitely be mine if I had done it—regardless if it was the truth. Nobody wanted to start a supernatural war, especially here in New Orleans. Tensions among the clans, covens, and dens were already high.

Was I even sure it was Nora? The scent of hemlock present was a huge clue, as I didn't think any of the other witches in the house used it, as nobody here had a real fear of falling victim to a vampire. They were just as intent on keeping the peace and avoiding a war as much as everyone else was, it seemed. But the magical signature on the remains instantly conjured up Nora's face and aura in my mind. I didn't need a spell or magic to recognize another sorcerer's or sorceress's signature as it was ingrained in us naturally. I could walk into the kitchen right now and concentrate on every surface and tell you which housemate had touched what.

I paced some more, on a mission to chew off every last fingernail. I had to do something. The cat was out of the bag now, and I had a decision to make. Trying to decide on the right thing to do was stressing me out.

My phone chimed, breaking me out of my pacing. I dug into my purse on the dresser and saw an unknown number. "Hello?"

"It's Craig. How you doin'?"

I hated the little flip my stomach did and the way my heart began to race hearing his sexy voice. "I'm good, Craig. Why are you calling?"

If he badgers me about this witch business so soon, so help me...

"I was calling to see if we could meet."

My eyebrows went up. "I was just there. I'm still sorting through things."

"I understand," he replied. "We don't have to talk shop. I just want to see you."

My heart beat in double time. The fact he wanted to see me excited me, but I wasn't sure that was such a good idea.

"I don't know, Craig..."

"We can just talk. In public. Look, obviously you're being apprehensive. I'll be at the Bare Bones Café waiting for you. If you show up, great. If not, then I'll just order a bunch of food to-go and I'm sure Venom will be happy."

Weird, but I supposed going into a café and not ordering food would look weird, too.

"Okay, I'll think about it," was my reply.

"Hope to see you soon." He hung up.

Of course, I threw my phone down, ran straight into the bathroom, pulled out my makeup box, and began freshening myself up. No way I could let him sit there alone. Besides, curiosity had won over. What did he *really* want?

"Hi," I said, taking a seat across from him.

"Hello, Bloome. You look beautiful tonight," he replied with a grin. He had a steaming cup of coffee in front of him. He slid a plastic menu toward me. "Order whatever you like."

Without looking at it, I folded my hands over it and said, "What's this about, Craig?"

He chuckled after taking a very small sip of coffee. The small white coffee cup looked tiny in his huge hand. "Nothing sinister or ulterior motive-like. I promise. I just wanted to see you."

"But you just saw me," I said, feeling dumb because I'd just said that on the phone earlier.

He reached over and pulled my hand into his. "I know, but I wanted some one-on-one time with you. I also wanted to apologize."

I lifted an eyebrow. "For what?" I asked, curious.

"For the interrogation earlier. Viper gets pretty passionate about crimes and wrongdoings in general. He likes to get things taken care of swiftly to keep the peace. He doesn't like things hanging in limbo. He wants everything wrapped up and put away."

I looked down at my hand in his. "I get it, but y'all need to give me some time. I have a moral dilemma with this and I'm going to have to do some meditating to make a decision."

The server arrived at our table and asked what I'd like.

"Diet Coke and your most popular appetizer," I replied with a smile. I was hungry but didn't want to look at the menu, I was too enthralled with this conversation and didn't want to remove my hand from Craig's.

"You got it, darlin'," the lady replied and walked off.

"Thanks," I said.

Craig's thumb ran soft circles over the top of my hand, and that sent shivers through me. His touch was cold but was slowly warming as he held my hand.

"What's the moral dilemma? If you're comfortable sharing it with me," he asked.

I stared into his gray eyes. They were so pretty and unique framed by dark lashes, and I wondered if they had been that color before he'd been changed into a vampire. He was also being extraordinarily nice. Normally he was brusque and grunty. Well, except when we'd had sex… he had been both aggressive and gentle. I pushed the memory away before I was tempted to climb over this table and straddle him in the booth in front of all these people.

I didn't want to tell him everything—he could be just trying to be nice to get me to tell him my secrets, so I decided to give him just a little bit. "Basically, I think I know who the witch is, but I don't feel comfortable handing her over to be punished or even killed for money. When I agreed to take the ten grand, I thought it was more like a reward or something for doing a magical reading on the remains, to find who did it. And I was okay with that until I realized it was someone I knew. Someone I sort of consider a friend. Or at least an acquaintance."

Now, Nora and I were not close by any stretch of the imagination. She was broody and moody, and I stayed out of her way in the house most of the time. But she was a fellow witch sister in my same coven, and that held some loyalty in my book.

"We're not going to kill her," Craig said with a serious look. "We don't kill unnecessarily. We just want to grill her some. See why she did it."

"And if it had been self-defense?" I asked.

The server brought me the soda and I reluctantly took my hand back to quickly unwrap the straw. I took a big pull, enjoying the sweet, fizzy taste.

Craig watched my lips wrap around the straw and then licked his own lips before responding. "If she can prove it was self-defense, then no harm, no foul. The vamps had it coming. The problem is, we don't even know who these vampires were. That would go a long way in helping us figure out what happened."

"I can understand that," I replied, sipping on my soda once more.

"You have beautiful lips," Craig said, staring at them, and then into my eyes. "And eyes."

I laughed shyly. "So do you."

He went to grab my hand once more, but the server brought my food. "Hot blue crab dip," she replied, setting it on the table.

My stomach somersaulted with hunger.

"Anything else?" she asked.

"Nah, this is perfect, thanks."

I plucked up a tortilla chip and dug into the cheesy dip. I probably looked like a pig with the dip all to myself, but I didn't care.

Craig watched with amusement in his eyes as I ate.

"Don't you miss food?" I asked between bites.

He wrinkled his nose. "Not one bit."

I lifted a shoulder and let it fall. "More for me." I twirled the chip around until the cheese settled onto it and shoved it into my mouth as ladylike as I could. I was glad I wasn't one of those girls who didn't like eating on a date.

This was a date, wasn't it?

I supposed I should be even more self-conscious eating by myself in front of a man who clearly found food repulsive. But I wasn't.

Craig looked around the restaurant and lowered his voice a little. "Bloome, do you think you could use some witchy stuff on the remains and find out who they were so we can at least give them a proper burial? Our clubhouse has a lot of things, but we haven't set up a place to store remains, and some of the guys are getting anxious about getting them out of there. Bad ju-ju and all that."

I wiped my mouth with the napkin and thought about it. I could do a spell, or better yet get one from my parents. They could do identifier spells in their sleep. The way Craig was looking at me, and how nice he'd been, guessed I was falling even deeper under his spell, whether he meant to or not. Unable to resist doing something that would please him outside the bedroom, I nodded. "Yes, I could probably do a spell to find out who they were."

His face lit up. "Wow, that would be really great of you."

I agreed, it would be. But even better than me looking like the hero here, it would buy me time to figure out what I was going to do about Nora. Because as soon as they identified these three dead vamps, chance was they'd figure out who had killed them through good, old fashioned detective work.

"I'll head to the clubhouse tomorrow night. I need to make sure I have the right spell and ingredients to perform it. And I need to consult with a couple people." When his brow furrowed, I already knew what he was going to say, so I cut him off. "Don't worry, I'm just going to ask a greater witch to look over my notes and make sure I have it correct. I won't tell her that it's for vampires or about dead vampires. Remember, I'm still a lesser witch. I don't have all my powers yet, but I can do this."

Since that greater witch was my mother, I may mention the vampire thing in regards to my attraction to one, not that I was essentially doing a whole clan of vamps a favor. Well, I was getting paid, but whether or not I'd actually take the money depended on if I decided to throw Nora under the bus. I had to get to the bottom of all of this, and I decided talking to her first before performing the spell was what I was going to do.

After I finished my food, Craig paid the tab and we walked outside of the café. He asked, "Can I take you home?"

Since I knew what would happen if he came to my house, and as much as I'd love to spend the rest of the night rolling around in my bed with the sexy beast, I pulled up every ounce of self-control

I had and said, "I would, but I have my own car, so no need. Plus, it appears I have a lot of work to do."

"Okay, but next time we go on a date, I'm picking you up on my bike so I have an excuse to walk to you to the door once the date is done—like a real gentleman."

I bit back a grin and said," You, a real gentleman? That I'd like to see."

He swatted me on my ass with a little sting and I yelped. "Ouch!"

He leaned down and whispered in my ear, "I barely tapped you. Just wait until I get that bare ass of yours under my hand. You'll be red for a week."

A full-body shudder erupted all over my body. Craig grabbed my hand, walked me to my car, and then leaned down and kissed me all warm and sensuous. I was about to cave in and invite him back to my house but then I thought about all that awaited me and broke the kiss.

With my hand on his chest, I said, "Goodnight, Shadow."

He nipped at my bottom lip with his teeth and said, "Goodnight, red."

21

CH-CH-CH-CH-CHANGES

Bay City, Michigan – 1955

I woke up curled into a ball and in complete agony. Everything hurt. My neck, my stomach, even my hair hurt.

Blinking open my eyes, I saw three people standing around, staring down at me. "Who are you?" I asked, then slammed my hand around my throat, as it was so dry, I was about to gag. "What happened to me?"

"You don't remember?" one asked. He was the shortest of the three and was very pale. I looked up at the sky and saw a crescent moon and a few sparce clouds. Glancing around, I could see I was in the forest. A fire was burning in a campfire in front of me.

I pulled myself into a sitting position, then looked down at myself. My clothes were filthy and bloody. I tried to remember, as the man had asked me, what had happened.

"I don't really remember much," I said quietly. "Do you guys have a thermos or canteen? I need some water badly."

They all chuckled. "You don't need water, you need blood."

I whipped my head up and stared in horror at the guy. "What? No. You drink blood?"

The guy bent down and handed me my canteen. I unscrewed the lid and began gulping down the contents. It wasn't water, but it tasted pretty good and helped immediately drench the fire in my throat. Once I'd drunk it all, I replaced the lid and set it down. "Thanks."

He reached down and gave me a hand to help me stand. "You feel better?" he asked.

I nodded, noting that nothing hurt now. I just felt dirty and a little confused. "Yes, much. Now can you tell me what's going on?"

"What's your name?" another one asked.

"Craig Walsh," I replied.

"Well, I'm David, and this is Jim and Bobby," he said, all of them staring up at me.

I looked around the forest. "I'm trying to remember what happened and how I got here."

David pointed to a pile of disrupted dirt. "We buried the wolf for you."

"Wolf?" I closed my eyes and searched my brain for answers. Then, like a punch to the chest, I whimpered. "Oh, sweet Jesus. Saundra. The wolf. The man… he was a wolf, then a man. Then… he bit me… I shot you…" I looked at Jim. "Then, I died." I put my hands in my face, trying not to cry as I relived it all over again.

"Yes, you did shoot me, and then, yes, you died," Jim replied. "That's why we turned you. We saved you. It's been three days and you've awakened."

"Turned me… three days…?" I shook my head. "You saved me from dying without a hospital?"

"Well, you're technically undead now, but you'll live. Actually, you'll live a very long, long life now," David replied.

I sat back down and put my knees to my chest. "I don't want to live a long life. I don't want to live another day without my Saundra."

"I'm sorry, my man. What's done is done. You already fed, so that sealed the deal." David stared at me apologetically.

"Fed? No, I haven't eaten. I'm not even hungry actually," I said, staring into the flames.

"Yes, you did. What do you think was in the canteen?" David asked.

I shook my head. "I don't know but it was very tasty."

"It was human blood, Craig, and you're now officially a vampire. We just wanted to save you. It was the least we could do for you after killing that filthy wolf."

I whipped my head up and stared at him in horror. "Vampire? Surely, you're joking."

None of them were laughing or even smiling. Bobby pointed to the pile of dirt. "There are werewolves, you saw it with your own eyes. Why can't there be vampires, as well?"

He had a point, but it was too hard to wrap my grief-filled brain around. So I simply said, "Oh, okay. Well, thank you, I guess." I didn't really believe what he was saying was true, but it seemed I did owe these guys my life in one way or another, so a polite thank-you was all I could get out.

The trio looked at each other, almost surprised, and David said, "You're welcome. Now, c'mon, let's get you out of these woods and back to our place. We'll get you cleaned up and some new clothes."

"I don't think any of our clothes are gonna fit him, brother," Jim said with a laugh as he watched David help me up.

They all looked up at me. I had to be a foot taller than all of them.

"I think you're right," David replied.

I'd spent a lot of time in this forest but had no idea this cottage was here. As I was led inside, I saw a small fire burning in the fireplace and random furniture plus a television set in the living room. There was a kitchen off to the right and a hallway behind it.

"The john's just down the hall. You can use the bath or anything you need in there to get cleaned up. I'm going to attempt to find you some clothes that fit but we may need to go into town to find some," David said.

"Thank you," I replied, still leery of these men but also taking note that if they wanted to hurt or kill me, they would have done so already.

But hadn't they?

As I went into the bathroom, I closed and locked the door behind me. I gazed into the mirror set above the sink and gasped in horror. I had dried blood and chunks of tissue around my mouth, in my beard, and all over my neck. My blue shirt was stained black with the stuff, and there were large spatters all over my pants. These clothes definitely were going in the trash. The boots could be salvaged with some baking soda and water.

I inserted the plug and started up the bath, waiting for the water to get hot. Once it was full, I carefully stepped in and groaned at the hot water. A washcloth and bar of soap sat on the edge, and I quickly washed away all the blood and dirt. I found a bottle of shampoo and washed my beard and too-long hair with it, then rinsed it under the water. As I got out and wrapped myself in a towel, I made a face at the absolutely filthy, chunky, bloody water that was now circling the drain.

Feeling much better, I cleared the fog from the mirror and searched around for a razor and shave cream. I quickly located the items in the medicine cabinet. I flipped open the razor and began to chop off the long parts of my beard. I watched as the chunks of hair fell into the white sink. Once it was short enough, I put some cream on my face and carefully began to shave. Wow, this razor was sharp! It was cleaning my face up nice and smooth. Once I was clean-shaven, I rinsed off the razor and went to close it when I sliced my finger on its edge. I hissed in pain and ran my finger under the cold water. As I searched around for some bandages, I noticed the blood on the razor and became a little fixated on it. An overwhelming urge to lick it off came over me... and I did. It tasted like the stuff in the canteen David had given me—the human blood.

I couldn't find any bandages, so I gave up. Looking down at my finger, I became confused… the cut was simply gone. Which reminded me—where were the cuts and tears on my neck from both the wolfman and my new housemates? Surely not completely healed in three days? I searched in the mirror to find nothing but a clean, smooth neck. I pulled the towel off my waist and saw my leg was also free and clear of any cuts or tears.

Realizing that I really was a vampire like they had told me, I got a little dizzy, having to use my hands to steady myself on the sink. How was this possible? Man, what I wouldn't give to go back to having no knowledge about these things. In a matter of just a couple of months, my life had been turned upside down, and I knew it would never, ever be the same.

A knock on the bathroom door sobered me from my thoughts. "Yes?"

"Craig, I put some clothes outside the door for you. They probably won't fit well, but it was the best we could do."

I didn't know whose voice it was, but I thanked them.

After a few seconds, I opened the door and found a folded tee, a button-up shirt, and a pair of jeans. I looked at my discarded boxers on the floor and realized they could be salvaged but needed a good wash. The jeans fit around the waist but would look pretty silly since the hem sat about four inches above my ankle. Especially with the hiking boots. The white tee fit, but was snug, and no way would the dark-blue shirt button up, so I rolled the sleeves and left it open. I towel-dried my hair, raked my fingers through it a few times, and exited the bathroom.

The three sat on the sofa and grinned at me when I walked out.

David whistled. "Wow, so that's what your face looks like."

I put up a hand and pointed at my clothes. "I know, I know. But I look like a total square."

"Do they even sell clothes your size at Montgomery Ward?"

I shook my head. "Not really. I can sometimes buy skivvies and socks there, but I have to get pants, shirts, and shoes at the big and tall store."

"Sit," Jim said, getting up from the couch, along with David and Bobby.

I did as I was told and folded my hands over my knees.

"Listen, Craig, we're going to let you crash at our pad here for a while, because we can tell you had been living in the woods. If you want to keep living there, that's fine, but we wanted to offer you a place here. It's secluded and people don't bother us out here. You'll have to sleep on the sofa here until we can figure something out, because there's only three bedrooms."

I looked at the sofa and smiled. I would maybe be able to fit my torso and head on it, the rest of me would hang off the edge. "I appreciate the offer, I really do. I don't think I'll fit on this couch, though. You cool if I just sleep in a sleeping bag on the floor until I can find my own place?"

He looked at the other two and they nodded. "Sure, guy. That's cool with us. I'm glad you decided to stay because we have a lot to teach you."

I cocked my head to the side, confused. "Teach me? About what? Oh, being a vampire. I think I'm getting the hang of it already. I like drinking blood and my wounds heal real fast. Just like in the movies. What about the sun? Do I stay out of it?"

Jim nodded. "Yes, you do. Sorry, bud, but you'll never see another sunset again."

David punched Jim in the arm. "Way to be negative."

Jim rubbed his arm. "Just being truthful. He needs to know."

"Well, that's gonna be a drag," I said. "I lost my job at the factory when Saundra died and was having a hard time finding another. Now where am I supposed to find a job working at night? Everything's closed."

"Well, I work at the hospital a few nights a week," David said. "It gives us enough money to keep the lights on and us dressed in these fresh threads." He pointed to his clothes. "Plus, easy access to blood. I have a few bags in the ice box, but they're only for emergencies." He jutted a thumb behind him at a new-looking refrigerator.

The kitchen looked immaculately clean and new, so I asked, "What else do we eat?"

David shook his head. "Nothing."

My eyes went wide. "We can live on just blood? Nifty."

"Yes. And we're going to show you how to tap a vein and drink right from the source." Jim looked at his watch. "We got six hours 'til sunup. Let's eat." He motioned for me to stand as Bobby tossed my boots at me.

I followed them outside and we began walking through the forest toward town. "I don't think I should be walking around like this. I look like a dweeb."

"Don't be a wet rag. Nobody cares. Most everyone's asleep, anyhow. It's close to midnight." David looked up at the starry sky.

We emerged from the forest and found ourselves on a side street. We kept walking until we were on the main strip. He was right, it was very quiet and dark this time of night. I had never gone out after dark before my life changed four months ago. Then, I would stalk the beach once a month on the full moon, trying to find that bastard who killed my wife. Then I'd go back into the forest, into my tent. During the day, I would try to find a job, but in a small town like this, nobody would hire me. They knew I'd lost my wife, and instead of taking pity on me, or appreciating my experience at the factory, they figured I had lost the plot and was too mentally unstable to hire. I knew I would eventually have to move to a new city and start over, but I hadn't planned to do that until that wolf was dead… and now it was.

After a few minutes of walking, I asked, "Where are we going?"

"Nowhere in particular. Just waiting to see if any humans are around, so we can eat."

"Do you honestly expect me to bite a human? I can't kill

anyone," I said quietly.

David stopped walking, and so did the other two. "We will teach you tto feed without killing, but it's a skill. That's why all three of us are here tonight, to teach you."

I put my fingers to my mouth. "But I don't have fangs."

Jim chuckled. "Yes, you do. They retract when we aren't feeding."

Brushing my finger over my teeth and gums, I didn't feel anything out of the ordinary. Yet again, I'd just have to trust these guys. These vampires.

We kept walking for a while longer and were heading toward the not-so-nice part of town. "Uh, guys, we shouldn't go here. Lots of shady characters and ex-cons around here."

"We know," Jim said, smiling. "Those are the types that like to stay out late at night."

The sound of music began to float into my ears, and when we crossed the street and went toward it, I could see an establishment called Al's where the music was playing. As we got closer, I immediately froze. Something delicious-smelling drifted on the air and hit my nose. Immediately, I felt my gums erupt with teeth. Sharp teeth that made my bottom lip bleed.

"So hungry," I said, heading toward the bar like I was a zombie.

Someone grabbed my arm. I looked down and saw David's hand on my bicep. "Let me go," I snapped.

He shook his head. "No, put your fangs away. We need to look like humans in there. And you will behave. No attacking the patrons. Got it?"

I reluctantly nodded, and my stomach twisted in pain. I bent over and grabbed it. "So hungry."

"Maybe he should wait out here and we'll bring him someone," Bobby suggested.

The three of them looked at me, then David said, "Good idea. I'll stay here, you two bring us a couple of drunk broads."

I gasped when I saw Jim and Bobby race so fast toward the building, they were a blur. I stood up straight and pointed at them. "How did they do that?"

"Vampire speed," David responded.

"Can I do that too?" I asked, intrigued.

He nodded. "Yes, I'll show you when we get back to the forest."

The back door to the bar opened and an older man in an apron came out holding two big trash bags. He tossed them into cans and my fangs again erupted.

One second I was at the side of the building, the next I had my hands on this man's face. I wrenched his head to the side and bit into his neck like an animal. I didn't know how I knew how to do it, it was just instinct.

David was right behind me and gripped me by the arms. "Listen for his heartbeat, Craig. Listen."

But I wasn't listening. I just wanted to eat.

"Pay attention! He's dying, you nitwit," David said, pulling me off the man. He fell to the ground.

I gasped as I saw his white shirt now blooming red with blood.

"Oh, Lord. Did I kill him?" I asked.

Just then, Jim and Bobby came around the back. They didn't have any women with them.

"Couldn't wait, huh?" Jim asked with a chuckle.

"This cat is fast," David replied. "He was already feeding by the time I sped over here."

"Is he dead?" I asked again.

David shook his head. "No, I can still hear a heartbeat. But it's very faint."

"Should we call an ambulance?" I suggested.

"No," Jim replied. "He's the bartender in there. Someone will notice him missing very soon." He looked around and said, "In fact, we should scram before someone does."

David looked at me. "Run, okay? Try to keep up with us."

The three took off with that vampire speed. I ran fast but couldn't keep up. How did they do that?

22

SPONTANEOUS VAMPIRIC COMBUSTION

Shadow

Viper didn't know that I'd met with Bloome. That had been solely my decision and I planned to keep that secret to myself. The fact that she had left here sort of freaked out had upset me. I was glad she agreed to meet me at that café. Watching people eat usually grossed me out but for some reason, I found it cute when she did it. And when her plump, pink lips wrapped around that straw, it was all I could do to keep my straining cock in my pants. One day I would watch that beautiful mouth wrapped around me as she milked every last drop from me.

I wonder if she swallows?

"Shadow!"

I looked up from my phone, where I'd been watching cameras mounted around the Quarter, to see Viper heading toward me. We had all just woken up from sleeping all day, and yes, I was drinking coffee because it had become a weird human habit I didn't care to break.

Vane sat at the table with me and eyed my steaming mug. "That's pretty bad," he said, pointing at it.

Confused, I picked up the cup. The outside read *UNT* in black letters. In small letters underneath, it read *University of North Texas*. I glanced at him. "What?"

"Look at the handle. It's like a C."

I set the mug down. Sure enough, the handle was painted black and formed a C, which conveniently sat right in front of the UNT. I smiled. "Clever."

"Terrible," he said, biting back a smile. "Whose cup is that?"

"Fuck if I know." I took a drink from my cunt mug and decided it was my new favorite. If I had to guess, it was probably Jewel's because that was the type of humor she had, but she wasn't getting it back. I'd drink blood or coffee out if it every day now.

"Any news from Bloome?" he asked, getting straight to the point.

I shook my head. "Nope. She just said she'd get back to me. To us. Whatever. I'm sure she'll come through."

He nodded. "Good. The sooner we can wrap this up and give those vamps a proper burial, the better. MyAnna's gone nuts with wedding planning and it's all I hear about."

He looked overwhelmed, that V between his eyes deepening.

"Don't stress—broads love that shit. Let her do the planning. Just as long as the wedding's at night, we're golden."

He chuckled. "Oh, she knows. Got herself a wedding planner and everything. Came to me yesterday bitching about how the wedding planner advised her against a night wedding for several reasons, and how she'd had to make up reasons for it."

"I'm sure she wasn't 'bitching'," I replied.

He grinned. "No, she really wasn't. I love her so damn much I wouldn't care if she was. I just want her to plan this thing out and tell me when and where to show."

"I hear ya. I wouldn't want any part of that shit, either. Aren't you getting married in the Cobalt Room?" I asked.

He nodded. "That's the plan. We make it official, all the humans leave, then we have the turning ceremony. That, I'm going to need help with, as she's left that to me. So that's why I'm coming to you."

"What do I know about a turning ceremony? I got turned to save my life after a damn wolf bit me. I wouldn't have chosen this shit." I pointed between us.

"Same here... I had no choice, either. As you know. Fucking bitch vampire."

"Fucking asshole wolf."

We both chuckled. Then I thought of something. I snapped my fingers and pointed at him. "Hey, Face was turned by choice. Ask him. I bet they had some fancy-schmancy LA-style turning party when he became a vamp."

Vane's face lit up. "You're absolutely right."

I stared at my friend, whose stress seemed to have come down a few notches since he walked into the breakroom. "Can I ask you something?"

"Anything, man," he replied.

"Does MyAnna understand what it's like to be this? Are you sure she wants to become a vampire? I get she's doing it to be with you forever, but does she truly understand how much it sucks?" I asked gingerly, hoping I didn't piss him off.

He nodded. "I've explained the suckiness to her. I've told her horrible stories. I've explained to her that she will never go to the beach or anywhere else during the day. That she'll never get to eat that sushi and pizza she loves so much. She says she doesn't care. She wants to remain young forever and that her growing old while I don't isn't even a talking point. I told her I'd love her for the next sixty or seventy years and take care of her, even when she's old, wrinkled, and gray. She said no way... it's not going to happen. Trust me, brother, I've tried so hard to talk her out of it. She won't hear me."

I thought about Bloome and had a feeling she wouldn't be the same way as MyAnna. The way she talked about vampires and how they seemed to disgust her told me she would never agree to be turned. I couldn't do it, anyway. Kovah would kill her.

"Well, you can't say you didn't try," I told him as I stood up. I washed the mug in the sink and turned around, wiping my hands on a towel when I was done. "By the way, when is the wedding-slash-turning ceremony?"

"Next month," he replied. "It's on a Saturday but I can't remember which one."

From what little I knew about women, I knew enough to know that he'd better memorize that date. I remember Saundra planning our wedding and she'd been pretty nuts about choosing a date and making sure I remembered.

"Well, you better find out and put it in that device of yours before you find yourself in the doghouse." I pointed at his phone.

"I'm gonna be in the doghouse just for asking her the wedding date again," he muttered.

I patted him on the shoulder with a chuckle before exiting the breakroom. "Text it to me so I don't have to share the doghouse with you if I forget to show."

Which was a joke since I spent every night in the Cobalt Room anyway. We all did.

We parked our bikes across the from the famous cathedral and walked on foot into the Quarter. We'd received a tip on the anonymous text tip line that two vampires had been killed by a "woman using magic to make them explode." When I'd read it, my whole body shuddered in revulsion. The tipster had said they witnessed it behind a bar on Dauphine Street, which was eerily close to Zombies, just a few businesses down.

Viper, Phoenix, Face, and I approached the back alley carefully. None of us wanted to be spontaneously combusted by a witch. After a human threw trash into one of the many dumpsters and went back inside the establishment, we waited to see if anyone would come out.

"Hey, fun fact. My very first feed as a vamp was on a cat doing that exact same thing. He was out dumping trash and I pounced on him. I had no idea what I was doing. I was so damn hungry."

"Ew," Face said. "The smell of trash and filth wasn't repulsive to you?"

I rolled my eyes. "I didn't smell trash. All I smelled was human. He was delicious, by the way."

Viper cocked an eyebrow at me. "You never told me that."

"Irrelevant to my story, but it kinda came back to me just now."

Phoenix chuckled. "I ate a witch for my first meal."

"Yeah, here's my shocked face," I deadpanned, pointing to my expressionless face.

Viper and Face laughed.

"Let's go," Phoenix said, pointing at the alley.

We searched around the dumpsters until we located two piles of ash and clothing.

"Fuck. Same MO. Bitch killed them. Just didn't burn them."

"How is she doing it?" Viper muttered, picking up a red T-shirt reading *Alabama Roll Tide*. He held it up. "Look, no stab wounds, singe marks, or bullet holes. She has to be doing something supernatural to them."

"Tipster said she 'exploded' them. How? Without fire?" Face commented.

I stared at the shirt and said, "I don't know. I'll contact Bloome immediately."

I texted her: *Two more dead vamps in the Quarter. Ash and clothes, fully intact. Same MO, it seems.*

I pocketed my phone and looked around. The anonymous texter hadn't said when this had occurred, but we could only assume the murders had taken place sometime tonight.

"Let's question the staff," Viper said, pointing to the back door of the bar.

We went around to the front and walked inside. Young people drank and danced under flashing green and purple strobe lights. If I could get a headache, I was sure I'd have a pounding one after leaving this establishment.

"Hi," Face said, throwing a charming smile at the female bartender. "Have you been here all night, beautiful?"

She looked at him skeptically. I had to laugh. The lady was probably in her forties and didn't look like she took a whole lot of shit from anyone. "Yeah, I'm the owner. Why?"

"I'm looking for two guys. Both wore jeans. One had on a red Alabama shirt, the other wore a blue pullover sweatshirt. Ring any bells?"

We assumed the vamps were men by their clothing, but the pullover and jeans had been iffy. Could have been a woman, but in all my years, female vamps dressed more… provocatively, especially when they were going into bars to attract men to feed from.

"No, not that I can recall," the bartender replied. "But I see so many people in here, I don't pay attention to what they're wearing. Only what they're drinkin'. Why do you ask?"

"Do you have cameras in here?" Face asked rhetorically, since there were cameras mounted in every corner of the bar.

She wiped down the bar top and said, "Yeah, but they are shoddy, at best."

"Think I can take a look?"

She whipped the towel over her shoulder and folded her arms across her chest. She eyed Face's cut, then looked at the three of us. "What do you want with those people? They piss off your gang or something?"

Face cleared his throat and put on his most charming smile. "Ma'am, we're not a gang. We're a club. We track down missing people, and we would very much like to find these two. Any information you could give us would be kindly appreciated." I watched as he slid a hundred dollar bill her way.

She looked around before snatching it up and shoving it between her tits into the very low-cut shirt she wore. "C'mon."

We followed her into the back room where she pointed at a computer. "All the camera shit is on there. The icon is blue, I don't know what it's called. There's no password on the computer. Have at it."

With that, she walked back into the front of the bar and left us alone. I stood watch with Phoenix to make sure nobody came back here.

After a few keystrokes, Face was scrolling through hundreds of videos. He found the ones dated for today and began clicking on each one.

"Fast forward to tonight," Viper said.

Face wanted to roll his eyes, I could tell, but refrained. He froze it on two men wearing the matching clothing. Their eyes shone white in the camera's lens, like most vampires'.

"There," Viper said. "Zoom in."

Face clicked some buttons and we saw their faces close up. Viper looked at us. "Anyone recognize them?"

I shook my head. "Nope, but it's not like I've lived here that long."

"Me either," Phoenix replied.

"Play the video," Viper commanded.

Face clicked the play icon and we watched as the two male vampires ordered drinks and sat in a corner table, conversing with each other. Not too much later, a female with a hood over her head, wearing all dark clothing, approached the table. There was no sound, but whatever she said had them abandoning their drinks and following her out back. It must have a been a good line, because the two fist-bumped each other behind her back as if they were in for a major score.

The trio disappeared from the camera's view.

"Any cameras in the back alley?" Viper asked, sounding excited.

Face scrolled quickly through the rest of the feeds but none of them had an outside view. "Doesn't seem like it, boss."

"Hey, go back to the woman. Freeze it and see if you can print it or email it to me," I said, an idea forming in my head.

"No printer," Face muttered as he took a screenshot from the computer and logged into his email account, sending it to me and himself. Then, he logged out and completely reset the computer back to its original settings.

It would be a bitch and a half for whoever used that computer the next time they logged on.

23

CONFESSIONS

Bloome

Well, that had gone easier than planned. My mom, seeming to beam with pride over our video chat, told me the identifier spell had been written perfectly.

"It's different once you're standing over the remains, but the spell is exactly the same. The victim's name will pop into your head, and after that, you just let the police do the rest of the work."

"Thanks, Mom," I replied.

Her face went serious. "Honey, please be careful, though. Don't go offering your services to the police as a 'psychic' very often. They'll get suspicious and if you're ever wrong, even once, they'll completely discount and discredit you." She looked angry. "Trust me, I know."

I smiled warmly at her. "I know, Ma. It's just this once. I promise."

She relaxed, sliding some auburn hair behind her ear before snapping on a huge gold clip-on earring. "Good. Now, I gotta go. Dad and I are late for this charity thing." She half rolled her eyes with a knowing smile, because I knew the people she hung out with loved to throw big, lavish parties in the name of "charity." She never missed a damn party, though.

"Love you, kid," my dad said, popping into the video over Mom's shoulder, adjusting his tuxedo's tie.

"Love you, too, Daddy," I said with a smile.

They both blew me kisses and ended the chat.

It was pretty ridiculous for me to video chat with them when they just lived a few miles away in my childhood home on the outskirts of the big city. They constantly fussed over me living so close to the French Quarter, but I was young, and this was fun for me. It sucked I had to have roommates to keep up the rent, but my parents didn't need to know that. They'd met Brantley and Skyla, but I had yet to introduce them to Nora or the other two who lived here. They would balk at me, saying that if I needed five roommates that I should ask them for more money.

I didn't want to, though. Sure, at twenty-six, I should be working some menial job, but I wasn't. My witch mother and warlock father gave me a three thousand a month allowance, telling me to keep studying on becoming a greater witch. Then they would cut me off once I did, and I would have to earn my own money. Age thirty was a little less than four years away and I knew I had to do something. So, I kept five roommates, paid my fair share of the rent, spent probably a bit too much on makeup and shoes, and socked the rest away into a bank account for a house. Which was why I really needed the ten grand the Nighthawks were offering me. I loved my parents but hated the control they had over me. Even if I somewhat had allowed it to happen. I'd realized a few months ago that I had let this shit go too far. I was twenty-six… I needed to be self-sufficient.

I tromped out of my room and down the hall to Nora's. With more bravery than I felt, I knocked on her door. She answered quickly, the door opened only enough to expose the sourpuss expression on her pale face.

"Can we talk?" I asked.

She maintained the scowl. "About what, Bloome?"

"I just… ah, have some questions. Please, girl?" I threw her the most charming smile I could muster.

"Questions about what, though?" she asked, holding strong with her face to the door so I couldn't see inside the room.

Her scowl and body language wore on me. I lifted a hand said, "Listen… just meet me in the kitchen. I need to talk to you. Woman to woman." With my dignity intact, I turned and walked down the hall to my room. After grabbing my phone, I stomped down the stairs to the kitchen.

I waited far too long, but Nora showed and sat across the table from me in the house's dining room.

"What do you want?" she asked with a bitter expression.

"Have you been killing vampires in the Quarter?" I asked boldly, pursing my lips.

Her eyes went wide, then she recovered with a blasé body posture and a smirk. "Why do you even care?"

I narrowed my gaze at her. "Because you're going to start a fucking war, Nora."

"War," she chided with a chuckle. "What the fuck are you talking about?" She crossed her arms across the chest of her black shirt with a big white skull on it.

"Three vamps a couple weeks ago, two more tonight… You know anything about that?" I asked, obstinate.

"I don't," she replied coolly, swiping some black hair behind her ear.

Something deep in the recesses of my soul told me she was lying. Confidently, I asked, "You sure about that? I mean, if you had killed in self-defense, surely that was justifiable. Right?" I smiled. "The coven can protect you."

Her countenance dropped, and she replied angrily, "Yeah, but if vampires attack humans, or witches who they believe are humans, shouldn't they be put down… dispatched like rabid dogs? That's self-defense."

I purposely paused a few long, uncomfortable seconds, then said, "Yeah, sure," I said, pretending to agree. "So why these men in the Quarter? Did they hurt you?"

"No, but they were vampires," she stated matter-of-factly.

I cocked my head to the side. "So?"

"So…" Nora raked a hand through her hair and shook her head. "What world do you live in, Bloome?"

"Excuse me?" I asked, shocked by her condescending remark.

"You heard me. You and your trust fund world don't belong here. There are actual monsters out here. Vampires and wolves who want to do real harm to us. You should get with the program."

I stood up, my hands planted on my hips. "And what program is that?"

Nora chuckled. "The real world."

My phone chimed in my pocket. A text from Craig… Shadow.

Craig: *Does this woman look familiar to you? She was last seen with two now-dead vamps at Frieda's Bar in the Quarter.*

Attached was a short, grainy video clip. Even through the grain, and even though the person wore a hood, I could see it was Nora leading two ordinary-looking men—vampires—outside the back of the bar.

I sat back down and turned the phone around, replaying it for my roommate. "Is this you?"

Nora watched in fascination as I played the clip. Once it was done, she clamped her lips together and raised her head in a haughty display. "No, that's not me."

Turning the phone back to me, I replayed it. Laughing, I said, "Clearly, it is you." I put the phone down and folded my hands together over the tabletop. "It would be easier on everyone if you just confessed that it was you."

"Where did you get that, anyway?" she asked in deflection.

"It doesn't matter. I'm trying to help you here. I can't sit here and let you keep killing vampires. Just tell me the truth."

"It's… it's not me. I was in bed all night, bingeing shows," she stammered before looking away.

Clearly more flustered than I had ever seen her, I chuckled. "No, you weren't. Just fess up, Nora."

She looked angry, her face flashing red. "Okay... look. Listen to me, those two were misogynistic assholes. Making comments about women all night, their asses, and breasts, and trying to guess which ones were more 'freaky in bed.' I couldn't take it anymore, so I led them outside and tried to get them to apologize for hating women and were being perverts. I bet they had raped women in the past, too. I could tell... I just knew it. They blew me off, laughing at me, then tried to leave. I told them they weren't going anywhere, and that's when I ended them. That's it, plain and simple."

Reining in my shock and horror, I cleared my throat. "No, it's not that plain and simple. You killed two men based on opinions and assumptions."

"They weren't men!" she snapped. "They were vampires. Filthy, bloodsucking creatures."

"They were also *males*. It's not right, but some do talk like that about women. Especially if they're a lot older, like most vampires are. It doesn't make them rapists, Nora. You just wanted an excuse to kill more vampires. Why did you kill the other three?"

She hesitated as if she was scrambling for an answer. "They were following me."

I pursed my lips and sighed. "Are you sure? I think maybe you were following them."

Nora shook her head. "They were following me, so I ducked into Zombies."

"And?" I prompted.

"They had drinks and were feeding on a few women, so I lured them outside. Same as the other two."

I scrubbed a hand over my face. "Nora, you're not the law. You can't kill vampires for feeding. No, they're not supposed to be feeding in public like that, but that's not your call to make. You report it to the council, and we notify the vampires so they can do what they will with the information."

She stared at me obstinately and said nothing.

"Why do you hate them?"

"I just do. Are we done? Or are you gonna drag me to Iliana and make me confess? Because I won't." She folded her arms over her chest again.

"How are you doing it, anyway? Burning them?" I asked, knowing she wasn't.

She hesitated again and said, "I used a spell to explode the heart without touching them. Then they just turn to ash. Less messy that way." She actually looked a little ashamed but then I saw a smile begin to form.

I shook my head and got up to leave. "I'm sorry, but I can't let this go. You have twenty-four hours to turn yourself in to Iliana and the council before the vampires come and find you. They won't be as diplomatic about punishment as the council will be."

I left the kitchen and heard her yell, "Fuck you, Bloome, you nosy bitch!"

Shaking my head, I went into my room and dialed Shadow.

24

SCORCHING ATTRACTION

Shadow

I grinned when I saw who was calling and answered, "Hello, gorgeous."

"Hi, Craig," she replied, but I didn't hear the usual smile in her voice whenever I paid her a compliment.

"What's wrong, sweetheart?" I asked, concerned. I left the noisy club and went into the walkway between the clubhouse and Cobalt. It was the quietest area we had aside from my apartment.

"You busy? Can we meet? I have information."

"Of course. I'll swing by your place now," I said, patting my pants for my keys and wallet.

"No, I'll meet you," she said quickly.

I chuckled. "I promise I'll be a gentleman, if that's what you're worried about."

She laughed softly. "No, that's definitely not something I'm worried about. I just can't have you seen at the house right now. I'll explain. Meet me at that same café from last night."

"You got it. See ya in ten."

I ended the call and materialized outside near my bike. I started up the Harley with a rumble and headed downtown.

This time, she had arrived first. She was drinking a soda and looking at her phone.

"Hi," I said, sliding into the booth across from her.

"Hi," she replied. She looked stressed.

"Are you all right?" I asked, grabbing her hand.

"Coffee, hun?" the same server from last night asked.

"Yes, thank you."

Once she was out of earshot, Bloome said, "I know who killed the vamps, but I can't tell you just yet. I gave her twenty-four hours to turn herself in to the council. If she doesn't, she's all yours."

This excited me, but I could tell it pained Bloome. "This woman, she a friend of yours? You don't seem happy to have solved the mystery."

The server brought Bloome a basket of something, a bowl of salad, and held a coffeepot. I turned my mug over and she poured the coffee in. "Thanks."

Bloome waited for the server to walk off, then answered, "You're correct. The woman isn't exactly a friend, but I do know her and hate that she's doing this. And now I'm in the middle of it. I know I offered, but I thought I'd just be doing a simple locator or identifier spell or something—and I never dreamed it would be someone sort of close to me. I just feel… stuck."

I got up and told her to move over so I could sit next to her. The table seemed like it was a mile wide, and I needed to touch her, comfort her. She scooted in and took her food with her. I reached over and grabbed my coffee.

Linking my hand with hers on the table, I said, "I'm sorry. Anything I can do to help?"

"If we do have to turn her into you guys, just make it quick, okay?" She looked pained.

I used my finger to tilt her face to look at me. "We probably aren't going to kill her, but we need to know how and why she killed those vampires. So we can protect ourselves."

Bloome nodded then picked up some white dressing and poured it all over her salad. Then she mixed it around before poking some onto her fork. "She just hates vampires. She had lame excuses as to why she killed them, but at the end of the day, it boils down to just hatred and a weird sort of racism against the vampire race. I guess that's the best way to describe it."

"How did she do it?" I asked.

I'd seen witches and other supes hate us just because. It was usually because they feared us, as we were the strongest and fastest of all the supernaturals and that made them afraid. So her answer didn't surprise me.

"She said she used a spell to explode their hearts inside their bodies, which of course killed them, then they turned to ash."

"Wow," I said, "fuckin' savage. But this is going to be a problem if we get our hands on her. She'll just use that spell on us, won't she?"

She finished chewing and swallowed before replying, "Yes, but if I bring her in myself, I'll use magical cuffs on her. It tamps down magic in witches. My parents have a set nobody knows about. They don't even think I know where they are, but I do."

"Handy," I said with a grin, lifting the steaming mug to my lips.

"They are."

"So where is this witch now?" I asked, hoping for a clue. Not that I planned to do anything behind Bloome's back and break her trust, but I would like to know where she was. Keeping your enemies closer and all that.

"She's at home, I believe."

"You don't think she'll go on the run?" I asked, concerned.

She nodded. "She might but I already put a locator spell on her earlier."

"Smart and beautiful. I knew there was something about you I liked," I teased.

She grinned before biting into one of the fried things. She'd dipped it in what smelled like spaghetti sauce, and when she pulled the thing away from her mouth, a long string of white cheese wouldn't let go. She bit down into that and looked chagrinned.

I used my finger to clean up the excess cheese and red sauce on her lip. "Still had some there."

"Thanks," she mumbled through a full mouth.

She was so damn cute I couldn't stand it. I wrapped my arm around her shoulder and kissed her temple as I stroked my fingers along her bare shoulder.

She pointed to my tattoo on my left shoulder. "That's a cool tat. What kind of bird is it?"

"Nighthawk." I grinned.

Her eyes got big. "Oh! Your club's official tattoo? It's beautiful." She lifted up my short sleeve so she could get a better look at it. Then, she took in my other arm, which was sleeved from wrist to shoulder. "Those are beautiful as well. Explain."

Most of the tattoos were green with a few bits of color. "I got the snake scales to honor my friend Viper for taking me into this Nighthawks family. American flag because I'm a proud American, a Boston Red Sox one for my favorite baseball team, and the initials SW for my late wife." They were blended together on a green background of leaves and other nature-type stuff.

"Your wife died?" she asked, looking at me with shock and pity.

I nodded. "Yes, before I was turned. It was a very long time ago."

"Well, the tattoos are gorgeous. I want to get a few myself when I save up enough money." She paused and then said, "I'm sorry about your wife."

"It's all right. I've mourned her and moved on. I'm shopping for a new one now."

She gasped and I laughed. "I'm joking. But I would very much like for us to see where this is going. You can't deny this lightning-hot attraction between us."

She set her cheese thing down and wiped her mouth. "No, I can't deny it, Craig. You got that right."

"Would you like to come stay with me tonight? We don't have to do anything you don't want to. Just spend time together?" I felt like such a square.

"I would love it, but I think it's best if I keep an eye on our little friend. Locator spell or not, I need to make sure she doesn't try to run. It's easier that way."

"Smart. Would you like some company doing that?" I asked. God, I sounded so desperate.

She shook her head. "I wish, but if she sees me with a vampire, she's gonna lose her shit. Plus, I don't have the magical cuffs yet, and I'm afraid she'd hurt you."

"I can disappear pretty quickly, though," I said with a wink.

Her eyes got big. "That's right. How the hell do you do that?"

I lifted a shoulder. "Not sure, just came with the package, I guess," I replied pointing to my body. It was the truth. I had no idea how I could do it, I just could.

"Can you do it with other people, or just by yourself?"

That was a common question I got. "No, I can't do it with other people. I've tried to. They just stay and I leave. It was extra awkward when I tried it while holding someone cradle style. I disappeared, they fell to the floor pretty hard. I felt bad."

"Well, you obviously didn't know," she said with a smile.

"I also can't do it while talking on a cell phone. It drops the call immediately."

"Still a cool trick. Bet you never have to pay for plane tickets," she said, grinning.

I shrugged. "I wouldn't anyway, too unpredictable when trying to fly at night. Can't fly during the day, obviously. I don't travel much, regardless. I have no one to travel with, so I just stay here."

"It is a pretty cool city." She smiled.

Nodding in agreement, I replied, "It is. With some seriously beautiful women."

She paused the salad bite at her mouth. "Oh, I'm sure you've noticed them all."

"Only one's been able to keep my attention and make all the others fade into the background, though," I said honestly, brushing a stray red curl from her face.

She stared into my eyes and put her hand on my cheek. "You have beautiful eyes. Such a unique color. Were you born with them?"

"No," I whispered. "They used to be brown. Started turning grayish-silver about a year after I was turned."

"Weird. But cool."

"Just like you," I said, biting back a smile.

She smacked me on the chest. "Hey! But... you're not wrong." She leaned up and kissed me softly on the lips. I could taste what she'd been eating, and it was strange.

"That was nice, thank you," I said quietly.

She looked at my eyebrow and ran her thumb along it. "How did you get this scar?"

"Werewolf scratch," I answered quickly.

"That was very close to your eye." She cringed.

I nodded. "Yes, it was. Doc said the hair wouldn't grow back, and he was right. It doesn't bother me, though."

Bloome pointed to the food. "You sure you don't want a mozzarella stick? They're so good."

"I can, but then you'll have to watch me projectile vomit and I don't think I'd like to do that on our second date. Maybe like our fourth or fifth?"

"Uh, no, I'm good," she said, laughing.

We had such an easygoing conversation now compared to when we first met. We definitely had a scorching attraction, and I wasn't sure how long I could hold out before I put her over my shoulder and locked her in my room so I could have my way with her beautiful body for hours. I could tell the feeling was mutual but told myself we had time later. After this witch problem was resolved.

I paid the bill and walked her out to her car again. This time, I pushed her up against it and kissed her wild and warm. Our tongues mingled sensually, and I loved the feel of her arms wrapped around me. I picked her up under her ass and she wrapped her legs around me. I could feel heat from between her legs, my hard cock pressed against the area through our clothes. I raked kisses up her neck and really, really wanted to bite her, but I wasn't sure she'd be cool with it. I was about to ask, but it seemed she'd read my mind.

"Are you going to bite me?" she asked between kisses and breathy moans.

"Do you want me to?" I replied.

She nodded slowly. "I don't know. Does it hurt?"

"Only a small initial pinch, then it will feel very, very good."

"Okay, do it," she said.

Without wasting a second, I inserted one fang into her throbbing carotid. She hissed quickly, then let out a long moan, her legs and arms tightening around me as she ground her core against me.

"I feel like I'm going to come if you keep it up," she said between groans.

Oh, my God, *I was* about to come in my pants like a thirteen-year-old. I swallowed a few gulps of her delicious blood and licked the wound so it would close.

Gently setting her down, I boxed her against her car with my arms and said, "I'm gonna let you get home, otherwise, I'm going to rip your pants off and fuck you right here."

"Shit," she replied, out of breath. "Raincheck?"

I laughed and kissed her nose. "Oh, most definitely. It'll be worth the wait." I grabbed my hard dick to adjust it behind my jeans

She looked down at the action, licking her lips. "I can't wait."

"Bye, Bloome," I said, kissing her once more before opening her door and making sure she got in safely. I closed it and got on my bike, hoping my boner would go down before I reached the clubhouse or I'd have to take a very long shower.

25

CLOSURE

Bay City, Michigan – 1955

I couldn't catch up with the three. I was running as fast as I could but wasn't sure how I'd used 'vampire speed' earlier to get to the bartender outside of Al's.

Maybe I just have to visualize where I want to be and that's how it works? I thought to myself.

As I ran, surprisingly not running out of breath or fatiguing at all, I closed my eyes briefly and visualized the cabin. Suddenly, my body erupted in sharp tingles and I stopped running. When I opened my eyes, I was standing on the porch of the cabin, the tingles slowly dissipating. I had to hold on to a beam to steady myself, as I had just been running and my legs were still moving pretty fast.

David, Jim, and Bobby appeared in front of the cottage in a blur and stopped short like a bunch of stooges when they saw me, shock on their faces.

"How the heck did you get here before us?" David asked.

"I don't know. I couldn't figure out how to use vampire speed so I figured if I just kind of thought about where I wanted to be, it would help me achieve it. Guess it worked." I shrugged, even though I knew that couldn't be right. I hadn't remembered running at all. It was like one second I was on the street outside Al's, the next I was on the porch.

"No, you didn't beat us here by running, we would have seen

you run past us. You didn't," Jim replied.

"Then I don't know how I did it."

David ushered us into the house and said, "Sit."

Then he retrieved three bowls from the ice box and set them on the counter. He lifted the lids and poured them into cups, which the three of them drank.

"Cold, gah," Jim complained.

"I'm sorry I attacked the bartender and you didn't get to eat," I said genuinely.

"It's all right, we'll try again later. This will do for now." David lifted up the cup.

I stared at the trio, not knowing what to say. "Well, I guess I'll go get my camping gear from the woods so I have my sleeping bag and pillow for tonight. You good with me storing the tent and stuff here somewhere? It won't take up much space."

"That's fine, but first we need to figure out how you beat us here," David said, clearly not letting it go.

I shrugged. "I don't know what to tell you, man. I don't know how I did it."

Jim smacked David on the arm. "Hey, remember that cat, Fred? After he turned, he could disappear into thin air and reappear somewhere else like a damn magic trick."

Bobby snapped his fingers. "That's right. He was a real freak. But then one day, he disappeared and we never saw him again."

"Yeah, because he said he was going to New York to start a new life or some nonsense," David replied.

"Maybe Craig has that gift," Bobby said, pointing at me.

"Gift? Becoming a vampire comes with gifts?" I asked, confused.

"Sometimes, but we haven't figured out why some get gifts and some don't," Jim replied, gulping down the rest of his bloody drink.

"We don't age, is that correct?" I asked, curious.

"You are correct," David replied.

"So how old are you guys?"

"We're biological brothers, we were born in the early 1900s in Chicago. Our parents died of the plague when we were teens, so we were on our own. Once we became adults, David got attacked by a vamp who turned him. He told us about it, and we decided to become vampires too. It made our lives easier. We didn't have to scramble for scraps of food, and we didn't even have to look for jobs if we didn't want to. We could live on the streets and not freeze or fall victim to the elements. We did that for a couple decades, then found this little town. The people are nice and trusting and it makes it easy to feed. I hypnotized the personnel department lady into giving me a job as a night orderly, told her I had a lot of experience. So I do that for money and steal blood while Jim and Bobby keep our cottage safe and keep wolves and other things away. Stalks our nightly meals for us, too."

I could barely believe what I was hearing. These guys were nearing sixty years old and still practically looked like teenagers.

"How old are you?" David asked.

"I'm twenty-four."

"Well, I hope you like twenty-four, you're stuck like that forever." He grinned.

I didn't see how that was funny or even amusing, and the reality of what I'd been turned into began to really sink in. I felt sick. "There is no way to reverse this? Seems more like a curse than a gift," I groused.

The brothers looked at each other. "Not that we've found. We've tried asking witches for help, but they won't even entertain the idea, most won't even speak to us. They're scared of vampires."

"Witches?" I replied, alarmed. Nothing good could come of the existence of witches. But since there were vampires and werewolves, of course there are witches. Why wouldn't there be? I thought about what I'd read about the Salem Witch Trials and their hysteria over witches made a little more sense now.

"Yeah, just steer clear of them. They're cranky wenches most of the time," David replied.

"Duly noted," I muttered. They wouldn't have to tell me twice.

I excused myself and went outside to try to locate my campsite. I knew it wasn't far and the walk would give me some alone time to think. I had a couple changes of clothes in my backpack, I just remembered, and an extra pair of shoes, so that made me feel better. Then I'd have to figure out how to get more clothes and necessities.

Once I found the campsite, I could see the campfire was still smoldering from where it had been put out before the brothers brought me back to their cabin. Aside from the horrific amount of blood all over the ground, my stuff was mostly untouched. I took my time dismantling the tent and folding it as small as I could. Then I rifled through my backpack and found that everything was still intact. I badly needed to brush my teeth and go try to get a haircut. I wasn't sure how long I'd stay clean-shaven, but I supposed if I wanted to fit in with the brothers and look non-threatening to humans so I could "feed," I'd need to look as presentable as possible.

As I kicked dirt over the smoldering embers, I looked over at the mound of disrupted dirt. I shuddered, knowing a body was buried there. Hate started to bubble up, and I wished I could dig him up and kill him all over again. I had no idea why he said I'd taken Saundra from him, but I thought maybe I'd go talk to her family and ask about it. I was sure they hated me, since I was supposed to be her husband, her protector, but I had failed. They couldn't hate me more than I hated myself.

I trudged back to the cabin with my things, and they showed me a small closet I could store them in. I changed into my own clothes and then looked around. These guys lived simply and didn't have many things, so there was plenty of room in the closet. I supposed living forever had to be costly so they lived as minimally as possible. Something I surely would have to get used to. I also knew

I couldn't stay here. They could live in the woods like this, but I still craved to be around people. I just hoped I could control myself around humans because I wanted to get a job and try to live as normal of a life that I could. Thinking about David's job as a night orderly made me realize plenty of things were open at night, things that couldn't close, like hospitals and fire stations. Or bars, they mostly thrived at night. There was only Al's here in Bay City, but I would bet a bigger city would have more clubs and bars—better nightlife that would allow me s job with some normalcy.

Besides, being that I had vowed to make a life and family with Saundra here, there was no way I could stay.

First, though, I needed to stay with the brothers, at least for a few months. They had to teach me everything I needed to know to stay alive, and I was grateful I was a pretty quick study so I could go and start fresh somewhere else.

The following night, as soon as the sun went down, I begged the brothers to escort me to Saundra's brother's house. He still lived in town with his wife and baby, and I needed to know who this wolf was. Since their parents had moved to Ohio for her father's job, the brother was the only one I could talk to.

My new vampire friends waited across the street under the darkness of some trees as I rang the doorbell. I knew it was rude to call on someone after suppertime, but I really didn't have a choice. Damn sun.

Her brother opened the door and narrowed his eyes at me before turning on the porch light.

"Hi, Jerry," I said with a small smile and a wave.

He looked up at me, his brow furrowed. "Craig. What brings you here?"

Jerry smelled so good, I wanted to dig into his neck veins with my fangs, but I had to swallow down that temptation. My throat burned and my stomach cramped, but I tried hard to ignore them. Probably should have fed first.

"May I come in? I just need to have a short chat with you about Saundra."

He looked behind him, then to me. "Well, Patty was just cleaning up dinner, but I think we have extra." He opened the screen door and invited me in. I made a mental note to ask the brothers if we needed to be invited inside like in the movies.

"I've already eaten, thank you. We could just talk here if that's all right." I pointed to his sofa. I didn't want to be around his wife or baby. I couldn't imagine how hard it would be.

I swallowed hard as he ushered me to the sofa. I heard the baby cry and watched as his wife headed toward the stairwell to attend to it. She waved hello to me before disappearing up the stairs.

"I'll get straight to the point and then leave you to your family time. Did Saundra date anyone before me?" I asked.

Jerry was only two years younger than Saundra, and I hoped he'd remember.

He furrowed his brow again as he sat, folding one long leg over the other as he thought. "I don't think so. You were her first boyfriend. We were happy when you proposed. My parents were worried about leaving her here alone. They wanted her to come with."

I nodded. "I know that. It's why I proposed when I did. I mean, I was going to marry her eventually, but just pushed it up sooner."

"Why are you asking about past boyfriends?"

I cleared my throat and prepared my lie. "A thin, pale man with black hair and shifty eyes has been threatening me. Saying I took Saundra away from him. I've told him to leave me alone and let me grieve in peace, but he says I stole her away. That she was supposed to be his, not mine. I haven't gotten his name, as I threaten to rough him up if he doesn't leave me alone and he runs off. So I thought I'd ask you."

He looked down, his fingers to his lips, and said, "I don't know who that could be. She didn't date anyone in high school at all."

Disappointed, but hoping he'd remember something, I said, "What about after high school?"

He looked up, his eyes wide, and he snapped his fingers. "You know, her manager at the ice cream shop, Wilbur, he looks like that. Shifty eyes for sure. It could be he had a thing for Saundra."

"She never said anything about him making passes at her or creeping her out?" I asked.

"Nope, but his picture's in the lobby of the ice cream shop if you go there tomorrow, it's right there as soon as you walk in on the right side of the wall. Manager of the Month or some nonsense." He grinned weakly.

I stood and put my hand out to shake. "Okay, thank you, Jerry. You've been helpful. Congratulations on the new baby, by the way."

"Thanks," he replied, pulling his hand back quickly. "Your hand is really cold. In fact, where's your coat?" he asked.

I jutted a thumb behind me. "Left it in the car."

He walked me to the door and said, "How are you doing otherwise? You okay?"

I smiled sadly. "I am. Just having a hard time getting a job. Spending a month in the nut house didn't help. Probably gonna be leaving town soon, start over and all that. So if I don't see you again, take care of yourself." I gave him a small salute and left his house.

"How did it go?" David asked as they met me on the sidewalk.

"He thinks it's a cat named Wilbur who works... well, worked at the ice cream shop. His photograph is on the wall there. We're going to break in so I can see."

"Sounds like fun," Jim remarked with a chuckle.

Once we reached it, there was no need to break in, all I had to do was peer through the front window and I could see his photo. It was definitely him.

"Mystery solved. Creepy asshole," I said. "Bet Benny's Ice Cream Shop didn't know one of their managers was a werewolf. They're probably wondering why he hasn't shown up to work in four days." I shook my head.

David reached up and clapped me on the shoulder. "It's good to get closure. If I didn't say before, we're really sorry about your wife. I read about it in the newspaper. We knew it was a werewolf. We were trying to find him as well. Turns out all we needed to do was go get some ice cream. Or in our case, a milkshake." He smiled apologetically at me.

"It's okay. I'll move on. God apparently needed her up there more than I did." I tamped down my emotion.

"Indeed," David replied. "Now, let's go get someone to eat, then we'll break into the big and tall store and get you some new threads." He looked at my clothing. "Gotta be struttin' in style if you wanna hang with us."

I chuckled. "That works for me."

26

LET'S GET READY TO RUMBLE

Bloome

Disappointment flooded me when I realized that not only wasn't Nora going to do the right thing and confess to the council, she was, of course, going to go on the run. It was nearing morning, and I was tired, just wanting to go sleep for a few hours, but I couldn't. I had been secretly watching Nora all night. Her bedroom was down the hall from mine and the two times she left her room to go to the kitchen or bathroom, I snuck in quickly to assess what she had been doing. Packing a very large suitcase full of clothes, toiletries, a phone charger, laptop, and everything else she could fit. A large wad of cash lay next to a plastic envelope on her dresser as if she had been counting it. I'd left quickly enough and now knew she was probably going to take off once she thought the house was asleep. Like vampires, we stayed up at night and slept during the day. Nora had been extremely quiet the past few hours, though, and I was wondering if she wasn't getting some sleep since she had a long day ahead of her.

Little did she know, she wasn't going to get far. I had spent a couple of hours of quiet meditation trying to decide what the right thing to do was. Once I had made peace with my decision, I contacted Iliana and told her everything. I also suggested that we let the vampires get involved, as long as they gave us their word they weren't going to torture or kill Nora. She needed to be punished, Iliana agreed, and she said she'd contact the council and get back to me.

That was three hours ago. I sent her a text: *I believe Nora's going to be leaving soon. I need the plan of action asap or I won't be able to stop her. Please text back, I don't want her possibly hearing me talking on the phone.*

Iliana: *Call the vampires, tell them to head over there now. Only two allowed, though.*

Me: *No can do. Sun's almost up.*

Iliana: *Shoot, that's right. Okay we'll have to detain her ourselves and get her over to their warehouse somehow. Got any sleeping powder?*

Me: *Wait, they have two members who can go in the sun. I'll get back to you. Stand by.*

I closed my bedroom door and ran downstairs and out the front door, far enough away where nobody could hear me on the phone. I dialed Shadow.

It rang several times and I realized he probably just went to bed. "Hello?" he answered softly.

"Craig, our witch is packing her shit, we believe she's going to run today once the sun's up and we're all asleep. We could try to physically detain her, but it would be easier if we had some muscle. That guy with the sunglasses and that werewolf you have in your club, they can go in the sun, right?"

He grunted and said, "Kovah's a hybrid so yes. And Venom can of course. Let me get some things sorted. It might be a bit, so keep her where she's at, don't let her leave. We'll get guys over there. Don't worry, sweetheart."

I smiled at his term of endearment as I watched the house, making sure Nora didn't try to leave out of the back or front. "My hero," I teased.

"You can repay me later," he said with a smile in his voice.

I smiled. "Oh, definitely."

"What's the address?" he asked.

"My place."

He scoffed. "This bitch is one of your roommates?"

"Her name is Nora, and yes, unfortunately," I murmured.

"Nora… the same broad we interrogated in Cobalt a few weeks ago," he said.

"Yes, Nora told me about that. Same person, my roommate and coven mate." I sighed in sadness.

"I'm sorry, babe. No wonder this has been so hard on you," he said, sounding sincere.

I saw the front door open and said, "Gotta go."

I ended the call and ran to the side of the house. I saw Nora look both ways before rolling that huge suitcase out the door and gingerly closing it behind her. She adjusted the backpack on her back and began wheeling the suitcase down the walkway. I just now noticed an idling car across the street with a paid car service's emblem in the windshield. She waved to the driver.

I stepped into her path, and she screamed, hand to her chest. "Bloome! You scared me half to death."

"Where the hell do you think you're going?" I asked, pointing at the car.

"I'm moving out. I left y'all a note." She sniffed and lifted her chin before trying to move around me.

Unfortunately for her, she was tiny, and I was about five-foot-seven with some muscle. Plus, she had the suitcase and backpack.

"Fucking move, bitch," she snarled at me, her straight black hair curtaining her too-pale face as she scowled.

"No." I stood with my hands on my hips.

"I'm leaving whether you like it not. You guys hate me, anyway, so what do you care if I move out?"

I shook my head. "We don't, but what I'm not going to do is stand here and let you just move to another city to terrorize more vampires. You need to be held accountable for your crimes. You can't just kill people and get away with it."

She narrowed her eyes at me. "I didn't kill people. I killed *vampires*."

"Still not cool, and now we're about to have a war on our hands," I snapped.

Her eyes went wide for a second before she said, "You're lying."

I ran over to the driver of the car and told him to go, the ride was canceled. I handed him a few bills from my pocket for his time, and he took off.

Nora screamed in frustration and began fast-walking down the sidewalk awkwardly with all her belongings. I almost laughed, but I was too stressed out. Where was this wolf and hybrid? And where was Iliana?

Shit! I hadn't texted her back. I once again stood in Nora's path and dialed Iliana. "I've got Nora here. The others are on the way. I'll hold her as long as I can. Call Skyla and ask her to get out here—"

"*Volare!*" Nora yelled, swiping her hand in mid-air as my phone flew out of my hand and landed on the grass about twenty feet away.

My instinct was to go get it, but I knew she'd just run or disappear or something. Instead, I pushed her in the shoulders, causing her to lose the grip on her suitcase and fall on her back. The backpack broke the fall and I jumped on her. She kicked me off and tried to stand, but the backpack was making her off-balance. She shrugged it off and lunged at my legs, tackling me to the grass. I was trying to get her on her back so I could sit on her stomach and pin her arms down, but she got me first and I tried to buck her off. She slapped me in the face several times, using every curse, insult, and swear word in the book.

"Get off of me!" I screamed.

I barely registered the sound of a vehicle as it screeched to a halt.

"Ladies, ladies. Let's break it up, huh?" said a deep voice.

I saw Nora whisked off me by the big werewolf, and Kovah reached down and offered me a hand up.

"Thanks," I said, brushing the grass off my back and hair.

Nora screamed and squirmed under the wolf's grip.

"What the fuck is going on out here?" Brantley asked, running down the stairs in some ridiculous unicorn pajamas. Skyla was on his heels.

"Nora's trying to leave," I said, "to run. Even though she's been summoned by the council to atone for killing vampires."

Brantley gasped and put his hand on his chest. "You were the one doing that? You nasty, nasty bitch." He shook his head and looked up at the werewolf holding her as she struggled. He smoothed his hair down, looked at Kovah, and said, "You, I've met," then to Venom, "But who's this sexy silver fox?"

I chuckled. "This is Venom, and you remember Kovah. This is Brantley, warlock extraordinaire."

Brantley bowed. "Nice to meet you both."

"Get her in the van," Kovah said, smiling at Brantley then pointing to the white van still idling at the curb, both doors wide open.

By this point, my neighbors were outside watching the commotion.

"Sorry," I called out with a friendly wave and fake smile. "It's all good now. Just a little cat fight. We're fine."

"No! We're not! They're trying to kidnap me! Help me!" Nora screamed.

My next-door neighbor, Alice, clutched her pearls and said, "Oh, my. Perhaps we should call the police."

I ran over to her. "No, Alice, it's okay. Those two guys are the police." I pointed to Venom and Kovah.

"But they look like bikers."

Shit.

"Uh, undercover." I looked into her eyes and whispered, "*Oblivisci!*"

She looked momentarily confused and wandered back into her house, muttering to herself. I located my phone in the grass and picked it up. I dialed Iliana.

"She's on the way to the warehouse. Meet me there now," I replied.

"We're already on the way," she responded.

"See you soon."

After retrieving my purse and keys, I hopped in my little sports car and realized I needed to make a little pitstop before heading to the Nighthawks' clubhouse.

27

SCALES OF JUSTICE

Shadow

I gave Bloome a quick kiss and disappeared, materializing inside the back of the windowless van where Nora was chained to the wall by her ankle and wrist.

She screamed in alarm and I laughed. "Hi."

"Fuck, you scared me, too," Kovah said from the passenger seat.

Nora immediately began to utter something in Latin, and I knew what she was doing, so I clamped my hand over her mouth. "Uh, uh, uh. No you don't." I looked at Kovah. "Gimme some help back here."

Kovah climbed between the seats.

"Make sure she doesn't talk. She's trying to utter a spell."

"In Latin?" he asked, clamping his hand over her mouth when I removed mine. "She's been uttering something the whole time and then screaming like she was mad."

I pulled out the magical cuffs Bloome had given me and slapped them on both wrists. I'd had to slide the shackle out of the way, but kept her chained to the van wall, as well.

"Yes, she's trying to make your hearts explode, but she's obviously too dumb to realize you're not vampires and that doesn't work."

"But you are," Kovah said, looking worried.

"I know, but those are magical cuffs, she can't do shit but scream and cry with those babies on her."

Kovah removed his hand from her mouth, and she started laughing. "Magical cuffs? What, to weaken my magic? Urban legend, They don't exist."

"Well, you can see that they do. Bloome's parents are apparently collectors of all the cool, witchy things," I said, smirking at her.

"*Somnum*!" she yelled, looking at Kovah and me.

Nothing happened.

"What does that mean?" Kovah asked.

"My Latin's a little rusty, but I think it means 'sleep'," Venom said from the driver's seat.

"Looks like the cuffs do work. Byeeee!" I disappeared and materialized in the clubhouse right where I'd left Bloome, kissing her on the nose.

She jumped and put her hand on her chest. "Fuck! I will never get used to that!"

"None of us have," Viper muttered as he dragged a chair into the middle of the clubhouse.

"Cuffs are on, they'll be here in a couple minutes," I announced.

Two minutes later, Venom and Kovah dragged the screaming, kicking witch inside and plopped her into the chair.

"Try to get up and we'll duct tape your legs together," Viper warned.

"Filthy fucking bloodsuckers. You might as well just kill me, and then I'll see you in hell," Nora spat.

"Well, it's daytime and we're tired, so let's get this over with so we can all get some sleep," Viper said. He looked at Iliana and the other two witches she'd brought. "Do your thing."

Nora narrowed her eyes at the three witches but said nothing.

"Do you confess to killing five vampires in the French Quarter?" Iliana asked. She wore some fancy, colorful priest robe-looking thing and a lot of jewelry.

"Five?" Nora said, now laughing. "Sure, I'll confess to five."

What the fuck...

"How many, young lady?" Iliana demanded. "I can make you tell the truth while you wear those cuffs." She pointed to the magical handcuffs still secured around her wrists.

"We can make you do lots of things while you wear those," Bloome commented, her arms folded across her chest. "I once saw my parents make a couple of witches quack like ducks for like twenty-four hours."

We all laughed. Even though I knew no one could do magic in the clubhouse, it was still warded.

She narrowed her eyes at the redhead. "Not funny, bitch."

"We'll see." Bloome inclined her head toward her hands.

Nora began trying to make her hand as small as possible and pull it out of the cuff.

"That's not going to work, they don't come off until I say they do," Iliana said.

That got me wondering—did they have a key or was it a spell, or what? Putting them on had been easy, but I would admit I'd felt a small, magical tingle as soon as they were secured around her hands.

"How many?" Viper demanded. "Your witch council may have patience, but I do not. I should kill you right now for murdering those five. So, you might as well fess up to how many more."

"If you're just going to kill me, why would I talk?"

"The council is going to punish you, we agreed to that, but you owe us a confession and explanation before a war breaks out. Witches killing vamps isn't going to keep peace in the Quarter,"

Viper said.

"Out with it," Iliana said.

Nora just stared at her defiantly.

"See those cages over there?" Viper asked. "We can just lock you in one of them until you talk. How long can you go without food or water?"

Nora glanced at the cages and then to Iliana. "You'd let them do that?"

She hesitated, then said, "Yes."

With a scowl, Nora looked at Viper and said, "I don't know an exact number, but I've been doing it for years. So probably a hundred. Maybe more." We all gasped, and she ignored us, looking at Iliana. "And screw you, Iliana."

Iliana, an older but very pretty woman, narrowed her eyes at the young witch. "Nora Lee, Lesser Witch of the New Orleans Order of Witches, I hereby sentence you to twenty years of mortal sleep."

Bloome gasped beside me. "Ooh. Ouch."

Nora screamed and stood up, lunging at Iliana. "You can't do that! Just kill me!" Venom and Phoenix plopped her right back down into the chair and held her there.

I noticed MyAnna was watching from the doorway to the breakroom. She looked scared and sad.

"What's mortal sleep?" I asked Bloome between Nora's screams and shouts.

"Think *Sleeping Beauty*. They're going to lock her in a glass coffin for twenty years where she'll sleep away her sentence under a powerful spell that will keep her body alive."

"Where a handsome prince will have to kiss her awake?" I teased.

She shook her head with a snort. "Absolutely not."

"If she's asleep, then how is that really punishment, though? Shouldn't she go break rocks in a chain gang or something? You know, real prison time?"

She laughed. "You can't send witches to prison, they'll just use magic to escape."

"But she can't escape the glass coffin?" I asked, intrigued.

Bloome shook her head. "No, she cannot. An unbreakable spell is put on the coffin and her body. She will wake up in twenty years, having aged and lost twenty years of her life. She might not be able to have children, either, as she'll be in her late forties by then. She will probably not know where she is or what's going on, as the coffin isn't monitored. It's just usually left in the attic of the council's house or somewhere like that. She'll have no help or consolation upon awakening. It really is a punishment. Like prison time, just asleep."

"Ouch is right," I replied.

"Harsh," Kovah said, smiling. "Brilliant, but harsh."

"Gentlemen, if you would be so kind?" Iliana asked Venom and Kovah, pointing to the door.

"Yes, ma'am," Venom replied, grabbing Nora by the upper arm and escorting her to the door.

"Make sure you get my cuffs back," Bloome called out.

Once they reached the door, Nora put her foot on the doorframe to stop them. She looked at Bloome and said, "Bitch, you better be looking over your shoulder when I'm out because I'm coming for you first."

"We'll both probably be grandmas by then, so that should be fun. Oh wait, no you won't be a grandma. Ever. You'll just look like one. Sorry." She shrugged.

"Fuck you, cunt! I hate you!"

I pulled Bloome to me as Venom and Kovah dragged the screaming girl out into the van.

"You're so savage," I whispered in her ear, pulling her tight against me.

"She's a bitch and deserves every year of that punishment. And fuck her for putting me in that position to begin with."

I brushed some hair back from her angry face. "You could have just ignored it. Pretended that you didn't know what was going on."

She looked up at me, smiling sadly. "You're right. I could have. But after meeting you, and your friends"—she looked around the clubhouse where the guys were standing around talking—"I knew I couldn't. I don't think I could have kept quiet regardless, and it didn't help that I couldn't stand Nora, anyway. But I had to do the right thing. I had to tell someone what she was doing. It was just wrong period."

"I hope you don't feel guilty for her getting locked away for so long," I said, rubbing my hand on her face.

She shook her head. "I don't. She's a sociopath with no remorse. She needs to be taught a lesson."

"Well, I hope she learns it after twenty years of sleep," I said.

"Let's hope." She sighed, resting her head on my chest.

"C'mon, let's go to my place and get some sleep," I said, grabbing her hand.

She followed me up the stairs, and we were both asleep, tangled in each other's arms, the minute our heads hit our pillows.

Something was tickling my nose and I blinked my eyes open to see red curls blocking my view of the face of my beautiful girlfriend.

Bloome groaned and craned her head back, looking up at me. "Good morning."

"Good evening, you mean," I said softly, smiling down at her sleepy, beautiful face.

"Same thing," she replied. "I gotta use the little girl's room. I'll be right back."

She'd taken off her jeans, socks, and shoes and slept in just a Metallica T-shirt and panties. I watched with pleasure as her cute little ass walked into the bathroom and shut the door.

I put my hand in front of my mouth to make sure my breath wasn't bad—which was silly because we didn't have those human problems, but still—and was relieved it was fine. My teeth could use a scrub, but I'd get to that later.

She emerged from the bathroom and hopped on the bed. She leaned down and kissed me, and her breath smelled like mint.

After I broke the kiss that had my already firm dick so hard it should be able to cut glass, I said, "You didn't use my toothbrush, did you?" Not that I cared, in fact, I needed to go buy a few extra and leave them in there for her.

She giggled. "Nah, just gave myself a finger scrub and a swig of your mouthwash, if that's okay."

"You didn't have to, but of course it's okay," I teased.

I pulled her head down toward me and kissed her soft and slow as she straddled me. I could feel the damp heat from her core getting hotter as my dick seemed to get even harder. While we kissed, I slowly ran my hand up over her flat, pale stomach and under her tee. While massaging her right nipple, I used my other hand to grip her hip as she rolled them over me. The scent of arousal she gave off was driving me absolutely insane. I pulled away from her mouth to toss her shirt off over her head. I threw it to the ground and then reached down and tore her panties off, tossing those away as well. Looking at her smooth, bare pussy, I groaned and ran my finger up her slit.

"Fuck... so beautiful. I want to eat it."

With vampire speed, I flipped her over, spread her legs, and began to devour her glistening wet slit. She yelped at first, then began to moan loudly. I inserted two of my thick fingers and felt her tighten around them as I began to suck and lick faster and faster. When she started to shake uncontrollably, I was rewarded with a huge gush of her juice into my mouth as she cried out my name, gripping the bedsheets tightly in her fists. I swallowed her juices, having never experienced that with a woman before.

I lapped at her clit a few more times before getting up on my knees, running a hand down my drenched beard. "Fuck you're wet," I said to her as she lay under me, panting, flushed red, and smiling.

"I'm a squirter, sorry. It's kind of embarrassing."

My eyes went wide. "The fuck it is! That was the hottest thing I've ever experienced. Can you squirt on my cock?"

She bit into her lip and nodded. "Oh, yeah. And I have." She winked.

Without breaking eye contact, I shoved my dick into her soaking pussy and moaned. "Oh, God, you're so tight, baby."

"That's because you barely fit, you beast," she replied, trailing off at the end as she craned her head back in pleasure. "Damn your cock is huge. Amazing and beautiful, but a bit to get used to."

"Stop, you're gonna give me a big head," I chided, pumping in and out of her slowly as I watched her beautiful pink nipples pucker in pleasure. I reached down and twisted one between my fingers as my other hand kept her thick, pale thighs open.

"You already have a big head," she said, staring at our connection as my shaft moved in and out of her.

While she watched, I pulled all the way out, slid the head of my cock over her swollen clit, then slammed back in as she squealed, and I moaned. "Fuck, you're wet."

"Yes," she murmured, gripping my biceps and staring into my eyes. "Fuck me, Shadow. Make me come. Make me squirt all over you."

Oh, sweet hell…

I began to stroke my cock in and out her, moving faster and faster, tweaking her nipple and leaning down to kiss her as I chased my release. All I had to do was feel her squeezing around me and squirting her juices all over my shaft, then I would unleash my huge load inside her.

I was getting very close and wasn't sure if I was going to be able to hold out. "Come for me, Bloome, baby. Explode all over my dick. He needs it. I need it," I said, staring into her beautiful blue eyes.

"Yes," she moaned, lifting her hips to meet mine.

I reached down and pressed my finger over her clit as I pulled out and then slammed back in.

"Oh, Craig," she cried.

Leaning down, I licked her neck and then bit into it, pulling her blood into my mouth as I continued to pump in and out. My eyes rolled back in my head at the myriad of sensations engulfing my body.

"Craig!" She squeezed her walls around me and gushed juices onto my cock, right as I stilled, spilling all I had inside her. I shuddered hard. I wasn't sure if I'd ever come that hard in my life.

I collapsed on top of her briefly, kissing her hard and then pulling out and rolling over. I quickly snatched her up into my arms, letting her curl into my side. She was out of breath, trying to catch hers, and the small part of me that had kept my humanity was also breathing hard, just because it felt like the natural thing to do.

I kissed the top of her head and squeezed her shoulders. "God, that was amazing."

"I can't even speak right now, Craig. Like, do you have a magical penis or something? I came like four times."

Pulling away, I looked down at her, surprised. "I thought it was twice."

"Nooo." She laughed. "I had a couple small ones but yeah, I'm definitely spent. I know we just woke up, but I feel like I need another nap!" She slowly got up and went into the bathroom to clean up.

"Me, too, sweetheart. Me too," I said as she closed the door.

She quickly came back to bed and snuggled into my heat. We lay there in silence, and after we caught our breath, we talked and talked and talked. It was strange. And nice. And amazing. And just… everything. I'd been missing this kind of connection with a woman for over sixty years, and after having it, I wasn't sure I would be able to let Bloome go if she ever wised up and decided to leave me.

That was when I knew I was completely and totally in love with her. I'd only known her a short time, but I had no doubt in my mind.

"I love you, Bloome…" I kissed her temple. "Wait, shit. What's your last name?" God, how embarrassing.

She leaned up on her elbow and stared into my eyes. "You do? You love me?"

"With everything in my body and soul, I know that I am completely in love with you." I was shaking, so nervous.

She grinned knowingly and leaned up, licking my lips and then my nose. "I love you more than you love me, Craig Walsh."

Surprised and fucking elated beyond all I could ever feel, I smiled like an idiot. "No. I'm pretty sure I love you more."

"Well, I'll just spend the rest of my existence proving to you that I love you more than you love me, woman."

"Collins," she said, kissing me.

"Soon to be Walsh," I whispered. Before she could respond, I pulled her into my arms and kissed her hard, fast, and sensual.

28

THE UNFORGIVEN

Michigan, USA – 1991

The brothers had been good to me. I'd had to make the best of a shitty situation, but they were great teachers. Taught me how to feed without killing. Taught me how to stay in the shadows at night when stalking for my next meal. Taught me how to break into a place without leaving evidence. They showed me how to hypnotize humans into getting what I needed or wanted. They encouraged me to experience the daytime on a very cloudy and rainy day so I could take care of daytime business without having to wait until the night. They reminded me to swipe blood bags from blood donation centers as often as I could in case of emergency. They even told me that we could be sustained on animal blood in a dire emergency. And most of all, they informed me that over my long life, that my memory of being human and all the things humans wanted would fade, and I would have a steady emotional state, showing me how to be a vampire without losing what humanity I had left and maintaining a humanlike existence.

My plan was to live with them for a few months and move on, but that stretched into six years. So, in 1961, I left Bay City and moved to Detroit. I was delighted to find out the car manufacturing plants operated 24/7 and was able to get myself a job working the graveyard shift at the Chrysler plant, earning myself a nice paycheck and a small apartment where I could lay my head during the day.

Love never came for me again. I didn't care, though. Once the hippie era hit, the women's lib movement, and the free love decade, I happily entertained any woman who wanted to share my bed for a few hours of fun. Gone were the prudish days of the 50s. None of the women ever held my interest for very long, though.

My job at the factory was enjoyable. I was able to make friends and socialize with people, even meeting a vampire or two I could relate to. They obviously worked the night shift like me, and it felt good to be around my kind. My thirst for blood never dissipated, as we needed it to survive, but I did find that I could feed once a week and be all right. Excuses as to why I never brought a "lunch" to work was met with explanations about how I didn't like to eat at night, and that seemed to quell the human curiosity.

Amazingly, I worked at that Chrysler plant for a full thirty years. I'd resorted to growing a beard and putting baby powder in it and my hair to appear gray, and often wearing low-sitting baseball caps to cover up my twenty-four-year-old face that should be looking fifty-four. I got a few inquiries from humans, but they never much argued when I told them I must have good genes. However, the employees at the drugstore must have thought I had a serious medical condition with the amount of baby powder I'd had to buy each week to keep up the façade.

The pension check from that job still got deposited once a month into my account and I knew it was definitely time to leave Detroit.

Not ever wanting to see another Chrysler name, I took part of my savings and bought myself a Harley Davidson Fat Boy, sold everything I owned, and packed up a backpack with a few changes of clothes and some photos. I took off up Interstate 96 and kept driving until I couldn't ride any longer due to the impending sunrise. That trip took me into Muskegon, Michigan.

"Cute town," I muttered, parking my bike in front of a small motel.

I got out, paid cash for two nights, and went into my room. Deciding the room was clean enough, I set my backpack down, took a shower, then lay down on the bed until sleep took me under.

Since I'd dedicated myself to spending two nights in this town, I was going to make the best of it—see what this waterfront town had to offer. After a full eight hours of sleep, I waited for the sun to set, then hopped on my bike and headed into town.

I found a bar called Shakeys that had many motorcycles parked out front. I parked mine right next to the group and wandered inside. All eyes cut to me as I walked in. Rough-looking bikers stared hard at me as I went to the bar and ordered a bourbon straight up.

I nursed the booze as I surveyed the bar. The bar was mostly inhabited by men in leather motorcycle pants and boots, wearing black leather vests that had a snake intertwined with a skull and *West Michigan Serpents Chapter* emblazoned on the back. Their names were on the front of their vests.

I was curious about what it all meant. Motorcycle gang, really? What did they do? Why the gang?

"What's up?"

I looked at the man sliding onto the barstool next to mine. His vest's name patch read *Cobra*. Pretty fitting for a gang member belonging to one called the West Michigan Serpents.

I was immediately guarded, but still kept my cordiality. "Hello."

"I'm Cobra. What's your name?" the man asked, staring at me with big brown eyes. His dark-brown hair was slicked back and greasy-looking. He had a shadow of scruff along his jawline.

"I'm Craig. Nice to meet you," I said, picking up my drink and not offering him a hand to shake.

Cobra signaled the bartender, and within seconds had four shots in front of him. "You like bourbon, I see," he said.

I nodded. "I do."

"This one's on me." He slid the extra drink toward me.

Weird. Was he hitting on me? To each his own, but I didn't swing that way.

"It's hard to catch a buzz, being a vampire, but we can at least try, right?" Cobra asked, right before shooting back his entire drink.

I whipped my head in his direction. "What the fuck, dude?"

He chuckled and set his glass down. "Are you new, or something? We can sense each other." He jutted a thumb behind him at the parking lot. "I saw your Fat Boy parked out there. Where you from, man?"

Was I really getting personal with this guy—this vampire? Obviously, he was trying to recruit me into his motorcycle gang.

But was that such a bad thing? Making friends with these vampire bikers would only be to my advantage—if I decided to stay here in Muskegon, and I hadn't even made that decision, yet.

"I'm from Bay City," I said vaguely.

"Cool. What brings you to Muskegon?" he asked.

I downed the bourbon he'd given me and shrugged. "Needed a fresh start."

"I definitely feel ya there. We all need that sometimes."

I nodded but said nothing else.

"You settling down here or just passing through?" Cobra asked.

Already getting annoyed at the inquisition, but not wanting to piss him off, I ground my teeth together and tried to smile. "Not sure yet."

"How old are you, man?" he asked, clapping a hand on my shoulder.

I looked down at his hand, then up into his brown eyes. "Pretty damn old."

"Aren't we all!" He tossed another shot back and stood from the barstool.

"I've got this weird fuckin' gift, that I didn't want, of sensing people's emotions, and I can sense you're lonely. And I'm sorry about that, but if you want a place to belong, the Serpents are always taking vampire recruits. Especially someone of your size and obvious strength. You'd make a great addition, and you'll have an instant family. We're tighter than blood, my friend."

"I'm not sure if a motorcycle gang is where I want to belong." I threw him a look and went back to staring at the liquor bottles lining the back bar.

"We're a club, not a gang, Craig." He patted me twice on the shoulder, set his glass down, and walked off.

Interesting proposition—and a very enticing one, too. I'd been in town like five minutes, and I was already being approached for membership in a motorcycle club.

I spent a couple more hours drinking and watching the sports games on the bar's televisions, and then I went back to my motel room once it got late.

Knowing it was time to sleep but not being able to, I spent the rest of the evening and into the day contemplating Cobra's proposal. Once the sun went down, I took my bike into town and wandered around. There were some suburbs with family homes, a downtown area with bars, restaurants, and businesses in a quaint setting. The people seemed easygoing, and the crime was low. It reminded me of Bay City and an easy peace settled over me.

At about 9 p.m., I once again found myself outside Shakeys, parking next to all the motorcycles. Taking a deep breath I didn't need, I wandered inside and found Cobra immediately. He was shooting pool with his fellow club members, men of all different sizes and races, a few women hanging onto those men—those vampires.

"What's up?" I asked, hooking a thumb into the beltloop of my jeans. I smoothed down my black shirt out of nervousness and raked my fingers over my beard.

"Craig, hello. Enjoying Muskegon?" Cobra asked.

I nodded. "Sure, from what I could see of it at night."

"Such a fucking drag, isn't it?"

I looked over to see a Black guy with the name Python on his vest. He grinned before shooting the eight ball into a corner pocket.

"It sure as fuck is." I pointed to his nametag. "You guys really take the snake names seriously."

"Yeah, I guess we do," he responded. "Python, lieutenant. What's your name, you giant fucker?"

"Craig," I replied, laughing as I shook his proffered hand.

"I think Craig wants to join the Serpents. Just sayin'," Cobra said.

I looked over to see a beautiful blonde woman hanging on him as he spoke.

I lifted my chin. "Maybe. Just getting a feel for the Serpent family."

"We are a tight-knit group. We look out for each other. What can you bring to the table?" Python asked, lining up another shot on the pool table.

"Well, what do you need, besides a giant fucker?" I grinned.

"Got any special gifts?" Cobra asked.

I contemplated showing them mine, then said, "Gifts? What, like this?"

I disappeared and materialized behind Python right as he took a shot.

He startled and his pool stick jumped. He missed the shot. "What the fuck!"

I shrugged and shoved a piece of gum into my mouth.

"Motherfucker, you are much too big to be just disappearin' like that!" Python said with a laugh.

"Elusive and dark, but predictable. Like a shadow."

I looked at Cobra. "I hadn't heard that, but you're not wrong."

"Stick with us, man. You'll find a family you didn't know you needed but one you know you want." Python put out his fist and I bumped it.

"I think I just might," I replied, feeling the warmth of relief blossoming in my chest. A motorcycle club might just be where I needed to be for the time being.

The West Michigan Serpents were good to me for ten solid years. Once I met Viper through the club, though, I knew it was time to go. Cobra got killed, sadly, and with Python begging either Viper or me to be its next leader, we just couldn't. There was something about my friend Vane that I knew I wanted to stick with. We went south to Louisiana and started up the Nighthawks.

The rest, as they say, is fucking history.

EPILOGUE

HERE COMES THE UNDEAD BRIDE

Shadow

"Oh, my God, she looks so beautiful," Bloome breathed from beside me as she gripped my arm.

Dressed in a huge, frilly, lacy black dress, MyAnna joined her husband-to-be in front of the podium inside the Cobalt Room. Everyone was here—me, Bloome, Face, Phoenix, Venom, Kovah, and his wife Mara. Of course, the prospects Jewel, Dash, Fox, Paz, Ally were here too. Even the BSI—Agent Bishop, his very pregnant wife, Charity sat among the small crowd.

Face was officiating, as he'd gotten his ordained minister license online to officiate the ceremony.

After some beautiful vows, Face was smiling from ear to ear. "By the powers vested in me by the State of Louisiana, I now pronounce you husband and wife. You may now kiss, and then bite, your bride."

Vane, dressed more formal than I'd ever seen him in my life in a tuxedo, gently grabbed MyAnna's mass of dark-brown curls and pulled her head back as he leaned way down to kiss her. After some soft kisses, he looked into her eyes, while using his other hand to rub along her face. "You ready, Mrs. Matson?"

She nodded and licked her lips. "Yes, Vane. I'm ready to be with you forever."

He bit into her neck, took a few pulls of blood, which was admittedly making my dick hard as I watched, and then removed himself from her neck. Then, he rolled up his sleeve, bit into his own wrist, and dribbled blood into her open and waiting mouth. She gagged a little bit but took it like a champ. Blood dribbled down her chin, neck, and between her breasts. I was sure some got onto her dress.

"Well, I can see why her dress is black," Bloome quipped, squeezing my hand as she whispered in my ear.

I smiled. "Definitely."

We all applauded and whooped and hollered.

"Reception is here, help yourself to the treats at the end of the bar."

There were ridiculous things like blood Jell-O shots infused with alcohol and bloody milkshake shots. And for the food eaters like Bloome, Kovah, Venom, Agent Bishop, and his wife, were regular finger foods and vegetable and meat and cheese platters.

As they all dug into the food and drinks, I went over and congratulated the couple. It would take three days before MyAnna became a vampire, and I knew she'd be falling into a very deep sleep within an hour or two.

"I'm so damn happy for you, brother," I said, clapping him on the shoulder. "You finding love has inspired me to do the same." I hugged Bloome closer into my side.

"Don't let his size fool you, he's just a big ol' teddy bear," Bloome said, jabbing me in the ribs.

I looked down at her. "Do not be giving up all my secrets, woman, or I'll have to punish you for it." I leaned down and nipped her bottom lip with my teeth.

"Oh, God. You two are grosser than us," Viper said, rolling his eyes while biting back a smile.

I leaned down and hugged tiny MyAnna. "You have a good sleep, girl. It's a wonderful three-day vacation. When you wake up, you'll emerge a beautiful vampire. Hope you had a nice last meal," I joked.

She smiled. "I did. Shrimp etouffee at Mulate's. It was

glorious."

"Well, I hope that wasn't today or else you'll be barfing it up later," I teased.

She looked at me in horror. "Are you serious?"

I laughed. "No, I'm not serious."

Bloome smacked me in the stomach with the back of her hand. "Don't scare the girl, you dick." She looked at MyAnna. "I'm sorry. Sometimes he thinks he's funny when he's not."

"Hey! I am funny."

"Funny looking," Phoenix said, coming up beside us. He looked at Bloome. "Are you sure you wanna be with this ugly fucker?"

She then smacked Phoenix in the chest. "Yes, I'm sure." She pulled her hand away. "Please don't set my hair on fire."

He ignited a flame on his palm and said, "I would never. Now, this guy, I may set his fugly beard on fire just because."

"I will stab you in your sleep if you even try," I said, making a stabbing motion with my hand.

Phoenix closed his palm to extinguish the flame and grinned. "It's not like that would be the first time that's happened."

Wow… this guy… he'd been through so much shit in his life. I thought being ninety years old had made me a little nuts. But I knew Phoenix was almost two hundred years old and wondered if I'd still be half sane by that point.

I shook my head, grabbed Bloome, and headed toward the food. "You need a woman," I called over my shoulder to my auburn-haired vampire friend.

"No, I do-on't," he replied in a sing-song voice.

I took a couple of blood shots, while Bloome made a plate of food. We bid farewell to Viper and MyAnna as they left the Cobalt Room to begin her transition during sleep in the privacy of his apartment.

Between bites, Bloome said, "That was a nice ceremony. I hope you don't think you're ever going to turn me."

That had come out of left field. "No, I would never ask anyone to succumb to this curse." I raised the Jell-O shot and slurped it down.

She piled a cracker high with meat and cheese and shoveled it into her mouth. "You know, there are immortality spells. I could do some research..."

My eyebrows hit my hairline. "Immortality spells? Now somebody tells me? Geez! I wouldn't have become an actual vampire if I'd known I could have just gotten a spell to keep me young."

She shook her head and smacked me on the arm. "You're so full of shit. You already told me you never wanted this."

I grinned at her. "You're right. I didn't. But it is what it is. Tell me more about this immortality spell."

Honestly, that excited me. Gave me hope. I loved her so much I couldn't let her go. I was willing to watch her grow old and die if I had to, and it would be worth a lifetime of unconditional love. The love I'd had for Saundra I thought was rare and one-of-a-kind. It wasn't. Yes, I loved her and was devastated when she died. But it turned out I had enough room in my heart to love again.

Bloome had showed that to me. She'd come into my life, and I was never going to be the same. If I lost her, I would shatter. But loving her would have been worth it. I just hoped we could be together for many lifetimes. And if we couldn't? That would be okay, too. Loving her for one lifetime would be worth every minute we lived it.

"I love you Bloome Walsh," I said, smoothing back some curls.

The cracker paused at her lips. "Excuse me, that's not my last name."

"Yet," I said with a grin. "But it will be one day. Has a nice *ring* to it, doesn't it?"

She cocked an eyebrow at me. "Speaking of rings... you better have something epic if you ever propose. I have standards, you know."

"Oh, I'm sure you do," I replied, leaning down to kiss her softly on her full, pink lips.

She pulled away and whispered, "Actually I don't. A plastic ring with one of those big, jeweled candy pieces would have me saying yes to you."

I felt like if I grinned any harder, I might break my face. "Be with me. Forever. Please?" I asked.

"It's already a done deal, Craig. My heart decided that weeks ago."

"Mine, too," I said.

THE END

NIGHTHAWKS MC SERIES

Viper

Shadow

Phoenix

Venom

Face

ABOUT THE AUTHOR

C.J. is a USA Today bestselling author living in Colorado but wishes she was someplace warmer. She loves the SF 49ers and has a weakness for expensive shoes. She's the author of over 40 novels and short stories that contain both fantasy and paranormal romance with kickass heroines and strong alphas. Having recently retired from a twenty-year career in federal law enforcement, she's looking forward to the next chapter in life.

She can be found on Facebook, Instagram, and on her website, cjpinard.com.

Use your device's QR code reader to get a link to all of C.J.'s books!

Made in the USA
Columbia, SC
16 September 2022